little big books
illustrations for children's picture books

gestalten

Marc Boutavant
Fresk
(see page 94)

introduction

THE ESSENCE OF COMMUNICATION

As one of the first storytelling media we encounter, picture books help us to comprehend the world around us and to decipher pictorial representations of its many denizens. With a minimum of text and matching images, they draw us into a parallel realm – and give us the tools to make sense of the one we are in. Pared down to a few core elements and storytelling devices, they represent the essence of communication. Yet how do children perceive colors, patterns, and depictions? How do they deal with abstraction? At what age do they translate the book's flat images into a richly woven, multi-sensory narrative? What are they afraid of? What delights them?

THROUGH A CHILD'S EYES

Well, while we cannot crack open the brains of our preschool protagonists, there are a few pointers when it comes to pictorial appreciation. Intent on translating the incessant input of their ever-firing neurons into something that makes sense, somehow, children constantly reassess the world around them. When the first synapses – and images – come together and reinforce neural pathways in our head, when we finally turn the camera obscura view of the world upside down to experience sight as we know it, when we learn to abstract from real-world experience to image and back again, when we start to color outside the lines of the stories in our (picture) books to fill them with life and imaginary friends, we literally interpret the machinations of society and nature.

According to children's book author and parenting magazine editor Clare Walters (see interview on page 225), "Newborns are attracted to strong outlines, sharp contrasts, and images with clearly defined edges. As they get older, babies love looking at realistic and colorful images of objects they recognize and love books that involve expressive sounds, such as animal or vehicle noises. By the time they are toddlers, they enjoy simple storylines as well as fun novelty elements such as flaps and pages that open up into bigger pictures. And when they enter nursery at around three or four years old, if they have been exposed to books from early on, they can follow quite complex storylines and interpret highly detailed images."

Easily swayed by visual magic – and easily enchanted by rhyme or reason, well, rhyme, rhythm, riddles, redundancy, repetition, and a strong splash of silly ridicule – children love the immediacy of picture books and their power to seduce and delight – and frighten. But most of all, kids love surprises and role reversals: like a round of peek-a-boo, where things appear out of nowhere or in the wrong place, subtle, subliminal pointers that unsettle our perception or upset the status quo (think childish parents, mismatched text / image, or timid wolf meets brave boy) kick-start a kid's brain, heart, and senses. At the same time, tricky subjects or nightmare topics – explained in a safe environment to take the demons of uncertainty away – can be processed more easily when couched in familiar characters and experienced in loving surroundings.

FRAMING THE ISSUE

Akin to a film script or a musical score, yet explored at the children's own pace and leisure, the dramaturgy of a good picture book therefore requires a thoughtful and storyboarded choreography of scenes, characters, storyline, and imagery, of cuts and perspectives, close-ups and wide shots.

Leaving plenty of scope and space for imagination, tension-enhancing gaps, or dissonance between what is said and what is seen, picture books thrive on the complementary, not redundant, use of text and image. Here, the visual sphere adds an open, interpretation-friendly layer to the text, allowing kids to supplement the underlying story with individual touches, and thus to create their very own narrative. Author Martin Salisbury (see interview on page 157) adds: "More and more often, authors are playing around with the word-image dynamic, allowing pictures to subvert or contradict the words and vice versa." Complemented by strong characters – temporary companions on the children's journey through the vagaries of life, from kitchen to wonderland – the final story thrives on the illustrations' unique style and atmosphere, which supports and boosts the main narrative on a visible yet subliminal level.

Rilla Alexander
Jorinde & Joringel
(see page 42)

THE KIDS ARE ALRIGHT

Often considered a valuable teaching tool – to convey and impart thoughts, ideas, plans, history, lore, practical advice, or vital life lessons – the resulting publications invariably affect our perception of art and design in later life. Like invisible friends, our favourite stories and images stay with us and, consciously or subconsciously, serve as a benchmark and reference for future ethics and aesthetics.

In an interesting twist, children's picture books are one of the few media bought not by their immediate target audience but by their guardians, i.e., their parents, grandparents, or friends of the family, who get to impose their own nostalgic, artistic, or pedagogic preferences. Yet while these well-meant "Oh, we know what's good for you" gifts might slowly collect dust in the corner, the wily charges often opt for sillier or more subversive fare (e.g., Werner Holzwarth's *The Story of the Little Mole Who Went in Search of Whodunit* or Adam Mansbach's *Go the F**k to Sleep*). And, lest we forget, kids are made of sterner stuff than we tend to give them credit for. While the horrendous demise of Heinrich Hoffmann's Struwelpeter, who loses his thumbs to the tailor's scissors, or the cheeky double act of Wilhelm Busch's Max and Moritz, ground up and fed to the chicks, might offend our adult sensibilities, most kids would not even bat an eye, while the mere hint of an ominous ghost might scare them witless.

In the end, it all boils down to experimentation: just as with food preferences, children love to discover their own tastes – although a rich and varied spread of visual offerings certainly helps!

FROM CAUTIONARY TALES TO POSTMODERN SELF-REFERENTIALITY

Historically speaking, we have come a long way since the dark ages of the Brothers Grimm's less savory tales, yet picture books remain a relatively new and nascent discipline.

After all, it has been argued that childhood is not a natural phenomenon, but a mere creation of society. According to research, children were mostly represented as little adults before the 16th century. French philosopher Jean-Jacques Rousseau is typically credited with creating our modern-day understanding of childhood as a brief sanctuary before the strictures of adulthood. Although parents certainly loved and cherished their kids in times gone by, practical considerations took predecence: children were expected to pull their weight as a supporting pillar of the household. And while Pieter Bruegel the Elder's painting *Children's Games* (1560) already hints at a lively culture of play, albeit with improvised implements, children were primarily seen as an investment in their families' economic future.

Against this background, the modern picture book tradition most likely arose with British artist and illustrator Randolph Caldecott (1846–1886) who first gave images pride of place and a key role in driving the story along. According to fellow author Maurice Sendak, "Caldecott's work heralds the beginning of the modern picture book. He devised an ingenious juxtaposition of picture and word, a counterpoint that never happened before. Words are left out – but the picture says it. Pictures are left out – but the words say it. In short, it is the invention of the picture book."

Back in his days, advances in modern printing technologies – vital for decent quality and affordable reproductions of lovingly drawn illustrations and images – helped to popularize the genre among creators and their audience as a welcome, colorful means of escape in the grim period after the Great War.

Following the Second World War, the genre not only blossomed, but proliferated in leaps and bounds with artists exploring a myriad of (modernist) styles. Incidentally, many established commercial artists and graphic designers switched their allegiance from advertising or publishing to creating children's books of their own, adapting the psychological tricks of their trade (simplification, slogans, stark styles, narrative highlights, distinctive protagonists) to spin a short, succinct, and seductive tale for their new preschool audience. Even iconic designer Saul Bass produced a children's book, as did Paul Rand – an artist not well known for loving children.

Increasingly bold in both look and outlook, the liberated 1960s and 1970s produced such irreverent and daring classics as Maurice Sendak's *Where The Wild Things Are* and Tomi Ungerer's *No Kiss for Mother*, but in recent years the adulation of childhood, the infantilization of those who have outgrown this age and status, has gathered steam with special treats, gifts, and indulgences. Martin Salisbury sums it up nicely: "We have progressed from cruel cautionary tales through Victorian sentimentality and excessive morality to cosy 1950s family stereotyping and postmodern self-referentiality."

Yet while most of the 20th century's key artists took inspiration from the "golden age" of illustration (e.g., adult-fiction illustrators like Aubrey Beardsley, Harry Clarke, and Ivan Bilibin) or Walt Disney's visual immediacy, these iconic precursors of modern-day children's literature are themselves worth a closer look. After all, they in turn influenced many of the illustrators featured in this book.

Dick Bruna
Snow White

TOVE JANSSON

Tove Jansson (* 9 August 1914 in Helsinki / Finland; † 27 June 2001), a Finnish-Swedish author, illustrator, comic author, graphic designer, and painter, might be best remembered for her loveable and well-rounded hippo-like Moomin trolls, but she also wrote plenty of grown-up literature. Born and raised into an artistic family, Jansson studied at three re nowned art colleges in Stockholm, Helsinki, and Paris throughout the 1930s. Her first Moomin book saw the light of day during the last throes of the Second World War – an idyllic escape from and antidote to the very real horrors of the world around her. Spurred on by the success of her pioneering art based on a diverse and multi-layered interplay of image and text, she went on to write a total of nine highly successful Moomin books, as well as several other comic strips and picture books. Yet despite her commercial acumen, Jansson's style remained decidedly idiosyncratic with a healthy mix of high-contrast b/w drawings, bold colours and occasionally bizarre compositions.

MAURICE SENDAK

Recently deceased illustrator, children's books author, and scene painter Maurice Bernard Sendak (* 10 June 1928 in Brooklyn, NY / United States; † 8 May 2012) added a new dimension to post-war children's literature with his seminal, enduring classic *Where the Wild Things Are* (1963), a tale of obstinacy, wonder, and bewildering companions who were loosely based on Sendak's own Polish relatives.

A cantankerous crank – and beloved icon – the artist staunchly refused "to treat children like dumb idiots," but rather considered them fully-formed humans facing real anxiety, pain, and suffering. Shortly before his death, he stated that "I refuse to lie to children; I refuse to cater to the bullshit of innocence." An unrivaled delight for the kids who got to enjoy his tales, the resulting stories drew on the folklore of his own Jewish-European background, the general terrors of childhood, and Victorian precursors like Randolph Caldecott; the lost child, the one stolen away, remains a powerful motif.

Initially met with scepticism and guarded rejection due to the uncompromising nature of his style and content – in the United States, his stunningly surreal dream journey, *In the Night Kitchen* (1970), was censored due to its display of nudity – and despite his disdain for the industry as such, the mostly self-taught illustrator went on to receive some of the genre's most prestigious awards, from the Caldecott Medal and Astrid Lindgren Memorial Award to the Hans Christian Andersen Award.

TOMI UNGERER

Oh, la la la! Decidedly grown-up chic and cheeky, French-German graphic designer Jean-Thomas "Tomi" Ungerer's (* 28 November 1931 in Strasbourg / France) books often feature below-the-belt humor with a political or salacious twist.

Possibly most famous – or notorious – for *The Three Robbers* (1961) (as well as for his iconic poster for Stanley Kubrick's *Dr. Strangelove*), Ungerer delights in "naughty" topics peppered with robbers, cannibals, snakes, and cursing. In his refusal to tone it down for the kids, the author and, most of all, illustrator likes to blur the lines between adult and child-friendly fiction – and occasionally pays the price for his audacity. *No Kiss for Mother*, for example, with its cigar-smoking preteens and a bottle of liquor at the breakfast table, saw him hounded by the FBI, got the book banned in the United States, and received the dubious honour of being named the "worst children's book."

Unwilling to pull his (verbal) punches, the self-described storyteller, satirist, Hans Christian Andersen Award recipient (1998) and "archivist of human absurdity" injected new realism into the genre and continues to surprise with both adult and children's publications.

BRUNO MUNARI

Versatile and multi-talented to the core, Italian painter, graphic designer, and commercial artist Bruno Munari (* 24 October 1907 in Milan / Italy; † 30 September 1998) also dabbled in sculpture, industrial design, poetry, and writing. A keen follower and proponent of the futurist movement, the press graphic designer and art director started to design children's books during the Second World War, originally as a special treat for his son Alberto.

Munari's main foray into children's literature, *The Elephant's Wish* (1959), perfectly pinpoints what makes his work great and truly groundbreaking: encouraging kids to literally get into the heads of their animal heroes (via hidden flaps), the illustrated book boasts a masterful use of colors, plenty of surprising details, and a deep, heartfelt sense of humanity.

LEO LIONNI

The very same year, fellow Italian futurist, graphic designer, painter, and author Leo Lionni (* 5 May 1910 in Amsterdam / Netherlands; † 10 October 1999) treated the world to *Little Blue and Little Yellow*, an elegant exercise in radical reduction and cut-up design that saw the light of day in exile in the United States, where Lionni earned his keep as a commercial artist for several ad agencies and a business magazine.

The first children's author to rely primarily on collage, the resulting mix of paper, oil stick, colored pencil, and mixed media proved inventive to

Annette Tison & Talus Taylor
Le Voyage de Barbapapa (Barbapapa's Voyage)

the core: Lionni would use whatever was on hand, e.g., tearing up magazines to illustrate a story for his grandkids on a train journey. With his generous – yet measured – use of white space and a distinct, clean font, he heralded a fresh, contemporary look that won the four-time Caldecott Medal recipient most of the genre's key awards.

ERIC CARLE

Fellow ad man and collage artist Eric Carle's (* 25 June 1929 in Syracuse / United States) iconic and irreverent late 1960s masterpiece *The Very Hungry Caterpillar* inspired generations of kids to "eat" their way through this delightful book – and children's literature in general.

Translated into an impressive 500-plus languages, this surprise hit was joined by more than 70 publications filled with Carle's naïve and colorful collages – less realistic, yet more imaginative and unusual than those of his peer, Lionni – and laced with a touch of late 1960s / early 1970s exuberance and swirling psychedelia.

Often charmingly crude, as if a child had helped him with cutting and placement, Carle's creations thrived on innovative, added dimensions and media such as actual lights to mimic fireflies, sound effects or die-cut pages. Filled with empathy and understanding for his young readers, these nature-inspired books help to counter the fear of the unfamiliar and unknown by explaining it all in friendly terms.

DICK BRUNA

Dutch author, illustrator, and graphic designer Dick Bruna (* 23 August 1927 in Utrecht / Netherlands as Hendrik Magdalenus Bruna) has become a veritable brand: cute and simplistic to the core, his creations – most notably the instantly likeable rabbit Miffy (Dutch: Nijntje) – have escaped the page to take over the world around us on shirts, bags, toys, and kitchenware. A godfather of character design with this precursor of many, many iconic and cartoonish creatures, Dick Bruna's influence on modern-day illustration and design cannot be understated. Reduced to thick black lines, basic shapes, and primary colors, his characters appeal at first glance – and populate more than 120 books by now!

Yet another artist with a knack for both applied arts and capturing children's imagination, Bruna, too, tried his hand at commercial art with posters (100-plus), book covers (more than 2,000), and promotional materials for his father's publishing company.

TALUS TAYLOR

Equally rotund, yet a few decades after the Moomins, Barbapapa's benign blob-like shapeshifters are the result of an, at first glance, unlikely pairing between U.S.-based biology teacher Talus Taylor and French architecture student Annette Tison.

A marriage of minds, cultures, shapes, stories, and perspectives, their 1970 creation soon expanded into a comprehensive series of picture books and animated characters suffused with plenty of naïve charm underscored by the early editions' sketched backgrounds and hot pink, ever-changing protagonist. Big, bubbly, and simply good enough to eat, their name derives from the French term for cotton candy, "barbe à papa" or "papa's beard," and reflects their cartoonish origins. Designed to serve as brief, delicious palate cleansers between program, the accompanying five-minute Barbapapa TV clips, translated into more than 30 languages, continue to leave their mark on an entire generation's collective consciousness.

CHARLEY HARPER

"In a world of chaos, the picture is one small rectangle in which the artist can create an ordered universe" (Charley Harper). A true farmer's boy and lover of nature, iconic 1950s modernist and graphic artist Charley Harper (* 4 August 1922 in Frenchton / United States; † 10 June 2007) loved the countryside and extensively traveled the United States in search of inspiration for his stylish and stylized prints and illustrations.

Harper's distinctive "minimal realism" captured the essence of complex, natural organisms with a bare minimum of elements, color combinations, patterns, and textures instead of realistic shapes. Beyond his science-oriented illustrations, the artist and graphic designer also tried his hands at a number of vibrant, educational preschool books, including the instantly charming *ABCs* and *123s*, both based on animal motifs.

TARO GOMI

Taroō Gomi (* 20 August 1945 in Tokyo / Japan) counts among Japan's most popular and prolific children's book creators, with more than 400 publications to his name. With gently irreverent titles and topics like *Everyone Poops* (1977), released as part of an educational science series, he continues to capture children's imagination. And often that of their parents, too!

Effortlessly flitting between simple strokes and complex shapes, yet firmly rooted in the two-dimensional realm, he invites kids to explore their own creativity and let their creative urges roam with plenty of detail-rich coloring books designed to entice the imagination.

On a more regional slant, some characteristic styles – and characters – appear to be the product of their culture and geography.

ILON WIKLAND

Swedish artist and illustrator Ilon Wikland (* 5 February 1930 in Tartu / Estonia) is the quick brain and sure hand behind the vivid yet delicate images that grace almost all of Astrid Lindgren's books (besides Pippi Longstocking and Emil of Lönneberga). Close to the seminal children's book author in heart, mind, and even looks, the talented illustrator enjoyed a long and fruitful collaboration with Lindgren that began with 1954's *Mio, My Son*.

Heartfelt and evocative, Wikland's filigree ink drawings and colored title and picture-book illustrations, usually sketched by pen and later colored with water colors, blend wide-eyed, childish innocence with darker subject matters. Like Maurice Sendak, she often takes inspiration from everyday life around her: some of the unsavory robbers in *Ronia the Robber's Daughter*, for example, were based on characters loitering in the line of a local liquor store.

LISL STICH

Fresh from school in the 1930s, Elisabeth "Lisl" Stich (* 1913 in Volkach / Germany; † 2000) swapped her solidly middle-class Bavarian background for an artist's grant in Berlin. Throughout the Second World War, she made ends meet as a freelance artist, composing "social studies" of the life around her as well as prolific newspaper caricatures.

Post-war, she enjoyed a close working relationship with German children's author James Krüss: With a boldness of stroke and lightness of touch, she would sketch out quick scenes, full of life, dynamic, and a little unfinished, or lend everyday helpers like trams, trains, and double-decker buses a decidedly human face.

Modern and Modernist in her approach, Stich remained ahead of her time: in an age where clarity and perfection ruled, she delighted in going over the lines, in quick dashes and unfinished vignettes that loved to toy with odd perspectives. The resulting illustrations show a small-town idyll, yet no small-town mentality, in luminous water colors, offset with pen and black ink.

VLADIMIR SUTEEV

Vladimir Suteev (* 5 July 1903; † in 1993), Russia's most influential author and illustrator of Soviet-era children's books, has shaped the lives and perspectives of generations of eastern European children.

Often dubbed his country's Walt Disney, the Muscovite and erstwhile cinematographer founded the U.S.S.R.'s animated cartoon industry with the country's first-ever animated film *China on Fire* (1924) and the first talking cartoon *The Crossing Street* (1931). Invariably inspired by animations in his later designs for papers and publishing houses, he delighted in their dynamic nature, their flow and movement, captured in his own "stills" of fictitious animations.

Suteev's later outings into children's picture books, such as *Two Tales About the Pencil and the Paints* or *Under the Mushroom* channeled his bright and optimistic style into everyday episodes and examples of matter-of-fact ingenuity. Witty, not moralizing, Suteev's stories epitomize the entertaining and educational slant of Soviet-era picture books – and even made it through the Iron Curtain, with more than 36 language versions to date.

KVETA PACOVSKA

Exceedingly experimental, Czech painter and sculptor Kveta Pacovska (* 28 July 1928 in Prague / Czech) oscillates between different styles, albeit invariably with a strong splash of color.

A graduate of the Academy for Applied Arts in Prague under Emil Filla, Pacovska turns children's publications into spellbinding (visual) poetry and contemporary art in book form. Taking a page or two from the likes of Paul Klee, Wassily Kandinsky, Joan Miró, and 1970s Polish poster art, she weds modern art with a childlike appreciation for wonder and turns classics like *Little Red Riding Hood, Cinderella,* or *The Little Match Girl* into aesthetic excursions filled with distorted abstraction, recurring check patterns, and plenty of graphic elements, often dominated by the color red. A startling experience – and a worthy one at that – her instant classic *One, Five, Many* (1990), sneaking Braille-like raised dots into the charming tale of a little bird teaching a hippo to count, takes a decidedly exploratory approach to counting with plenty of cut-outs, flaps, pull-outs, and mirrors to make the most of the medium's options.

TICKS, TRICKS, AND TRENDS

Today, the boundaries are getting decidedly blurred. On bookshelves around the world, the genre of picture books no longer differentiates between true children's books, comics, graphic novels, or publications that use naïve illustration styles and linguistic approaches to drive their decidedly adult message home.

While magic and mystery remain perennial favourites, many children – and authors – increasingly favor everyday topics, stories, and vignettes to reflect their own experience and existence, sometimes with an educational twist. Opening up new frontiers, more and more books touch on the less tangible, yet no less powerful topics of love and loss, birth and death, community and loneliness, albeit abstracted and simplified to supply a secure environment for these touchy subjects.

And although local and national folklore used to dominate and shape the aesthetics of many picture books, recent decades have seen a shift toward an internationalization with plenty of cross-border and cross-cultural licensing. Nevertheless, we can still discern broad aesthetic trends in large markets like the United Kingdom / United States (character-based, traditional illustrations), France (generous overlap between children's books, comics, and graphic novels), Scandinavia / Central Europe (strong narrative tradition with higher text content), Italy, Spain, and Latin America (minimalist and graphical approaches as well as examples of abstract painting), and Asia (often based on traditional techniques like water colors or calligraphy).

Meanwhile, nations late to the written language game – think parts of Asia, Australia, Africa, or South America – remain especially rich in drawn and painted lore, based on vivid recollections of times past, foes vanquished, and ingenious tricks that helped to ease and promote life and survival in trying times with glorious myths and enchanted fables. Exercises in ethnography, their contemporary picture book offspring snatch elements of this oral and visual history to weave their own vivid tales.

Attuned to these changing tastes, narratives, and market movements, open-eyed editors and perceptive publishing houses continue to play a vital role in the discovery and cultivation of budding artists – and the resulting creative process tends to be a two-way street (see interview with Kitty Crowther, page 33). Often taking a welcome long-term approach and view, outstanding editors – like Harper & Row's legendary Ursula Nordström who cherished, nurtured, and defended beloved recalcitrant geniuses like Maurice Sendak and Tomi Ungerer, among others – serve as headstrong and softhearted yet pivotal enablers who can set the stage and direction for an entire generation of picture books. And yet there is trouble afoot: pandering to economic trends in the growing – and increasingly competitive – picture-book market, actual contents, creativity, and originality might lose out, right down to the point where bookstores dedicate entire pink-clad corners to a monoculture of princess books.

WINNING FORMULAE

Out to restore the balance and bring quality to the fore, an increasing number of awards, seals, and official endorsements seek to serve as navigational (and sometimes promotional) aids for those who want the best for their kids. Analogous to, say, the market for fine wines or organic food, the genre of children's books now brims with many different labels, certificates, and recommendations, issued by a number of industry bodies and independent institutions.

While some are obvious ploys to draw the buyer's eye and wallet, others – from the Caldecott Medal (since 1937 for U.S.-based publications) and the Hans Christian Andersen Award (since 1956, otherwise known as "the Nobel Prize for children's literature") to the relatively recent Astrid Lindgren Memorial Award (since 2003, the highest endowned award of the genre) – have set their sights on loftier goals to further children's rights and the quality of children's literature in general.

Against this background, and characterized by an incredibly diverse and ever-changing mix of players and influences – from sophisticated contents, imaginative illustrations, and cross-cultural collaborations to digital multimedia versions, a bewildering array of awards, and the looming threat of mainstream marketing might – the future remains decidedly open.

LITTLE BIG BOOKS COME INTO THEIR OWN

In a climate of economic, cultural, and aesthetic globalization, with its multiway flow of information, goods, and styles, most of the examples featured in this book no longer draw on a local or folklore-based tradition, but rather concoct an international and individual distillate of what moves our (childish) hearts and minds.

Perched on this fascinating tipping point in children's illustrated literature, these creators and illustrators invariably have a very distinct visual slant: While some opt for an almost indecipherable degree of abstraction and minimalism in both style and layout, others find their (visual) devil (or sprite or gnome or duck or wolf) in the detail.

And while picturesque approaches still hold their own, bolder strokes and simplification also stake their claim. Pare it down to the essentials to give the imagination room to roam!

Yet no matter the style or level of experimentation: In the end, picture books remain a mirror of the children's world itself, with all its undiscovered mysteries. And we, in turn, might need the artist's unfiltered view to notice the magic all around us.

Sonja Commentz

P.S. Building on the genre's seminal pioneers whose works have helped to shift the genre's visual and contextual boundaries to make it the vibrant, ever-surprising, and sometimes deliciously subversive discipline it has become, there is simply no way to map the sheer breadth and wealth of illustrated picture books on offer, so we can only hope to showcase some of the best examples. In order to really appreciate the depth of a story, its accord of image and text, narrative and spell-binding atmosphere, and to grasp just how some of the more radical and abstract samples truly work, there is no quick fix or detour. Just get the book, grab a willing child, find a seat, and read the entire story together: turning the pages, cover to cover. And then start again at the beginning!

interview kitty crowther *32*
children's book author and illustrator

interview larry lempert *120-123*
jury member astrid lindgren memorial award

interview martin salisbury *156-163*
on the history, make-up and psychology of picture books

interview johanna brock-lacassin *186-189*
on publishing rights and licensing

interview claire walters *224-227*
on the educational aspects of children's picture books

O livro dos quintais
Author/Illustrator Isabel M. Martins/Bernardo Carvalho
First Published 2010, Planeta Tangerina, Portugal
Original Language Portuguese

bernardo carvalho

An Illustrator of 13 books, Bernardo Carvalho is a native of Lisbon, where he was born in 1973. Carvalho's book *Pê de Pai,* written by Isabel Minhós Martins, won the Book Art Foundation's honorable mention for Best Book Design From All Over the World in 2008. In 2009, he was one of the winners of the CJ Picture Book Award with his book *As duas estradas,* also with text by Martins. A graduate of the University of Lisbon's Faculty of Fine Arts, Carvalho is one of the co-founders of the Portuguese publishing house Planeta Tangerina, making books in which text and images work together and complement each other to create a beautifully integrated reading experience for book lovers both old and young.

CLIC!

Una bacchetta magica [1]
Author/Illustrator Antonio Koch/Gwénola Carrère
First Published 2005, Topipittori, Italy
Original Language Italian

ABC cercasi [2,3,4]
Author/Illustrator Gwénola Carrère
First Published 2008, Topipittori, Italy
Original Language Italian

gwénola carrère

Geneva-born illustrator Gwénola Carrère specializes in illustrations for cultural events, music, and youth. A graduate of St. Luc University in Brussels, she works mainly with silkscreening, painting, and digital illustration. Her publishers and clients include Topipittori, Bayard, Thierry Magnier, Albin Michel Jeunesse, Djeco, and Dada, to name only a few. Carrère has drawn several books for children, including popular Topipittori titles like *ABC cercasi*, for young children, and *Una bacchetta magica*, for slightly older kids. Her books have been translated into many languages, including Italian, French, and Portuguese.

Stuck [1]
Author/Illustrator Oliver Jeffers
First Published 2011, HarperCollins, United Kingdom
Original Language English

The Heart and The Bottle [2]
Author/Illustrator Oliver Jeffers
First Published 2010, HarperCollins, United Kingdom
Original Language English

oliver jeffers

New York-based painter and illustrator Oliver Jeffers published his first book for children, *How to Catch a Star*, with HarperCollins in 2004. The book, which was inspired by a moment star-gazing on a jetty, was shortlisted for the Booktrust Early Years Award for Best New Illustrator and won a Merit Award at the CBI/Bisto Book of the Year Awards. Since publishing this book internationally, Jeffers has created many more beautiful and inviting kids' books, like *Lost and Found* and *The Great Paper Caper*. Born in Australia in 1977 and raised in Northern Ireland, he has traveled the globe exhibiting his work everywhere from New York to Sydney.

4

1

Up and Down [3]
Author/Illustrator Oliver Jeffers
First Published 2010, HarperCollins, United Kingdom
Original Language English

Gelsomino nel paese dei bugiardi [1,2]
Author/Illustrator Gianni Rodari/Valeria Petrone
First Published 2009, Edizioni El, Italy
Original Language Italian

Two at the Zoo [3]
Author/Illustrator Danna Smith/Valeria Petrone
First Published 2009, Clarion Books, United States
Original Language English

2

1

3

Potty Animals [4]
Author/Illustrator Hope Vestergaard/Valeria Petrone
First Published 2010, Sterling Publishing Co., United States
Original Language English

valeria petrone

Valeria Petrone began her art education in her native Italy and then moved to London, pursuing studies at the Saint Martins School of Art. She worked in London as a freelance illustrator for several years. Although still maintaining links with publishers in the United Kingdom, she has extended the scope of her activity to include publishers in the United States, Japan, France, and Italy, where she now lives. In addition to her work in children's books, she has done editorial illustration for Italian and U.K. magazines. She illustrates books for a variety of children's authors, including *Ducks in Muck* by Lori Haskins, *Say Cheese!* by Nancy Smiler Levison, and *Uh-Oh!* by Dane Bauer.

1

3

Animal Colours! [1,2]
Author/Illustrator Nicola Killen
First Published 2012, Egmont UK, United Kingdom
Original Language English

Fluff and Billy Do Everything Together! [3,4]
Author/Illustrator Nicola Killen
First Published 2011, Egmont UK, United Kingdom
Original Language English

nicola killen

Young British illustrator Nicola Killen graduated with a master's in children's book illustration from the Cambridge School of Art at Anglia Ruskin University. She finished her first children's book in 2010 with the publishers Egmont UK. The book, titled *Not Me!*, was quickly followed by *Fluff and Billy Do Everything Together*, *Animal Opposites*, *Animal Noises*, *Animal Numbers*, and *Animal Colours*, all from Egmont. Additionally, Killen received Egmont's 2009 New Talent Award for her fresh and observant work. Killen has also worked in the art department at International TV and been a designer for International Greetings and Watermark Publishing.

Woooo [1,2]
Author/Illustrator Gerry Turley
First Published 2013, David Fickling Books (RHCB), United Kingdom
Original Language English

Mac & Mamma [3,4]
Author/Illustrator Gerry Turley
Unpublished
Original Language English

gerry turley

Since studying illustration at the Glasgow School of Art and the Royal College of Art, Gerry Turley has worked in many areas of illustration, with a particular love for drawing from like, letterpress, and silkscreening. The artist's many clients include Pentagram, Egmont Press, Met Studio, and Puffin Books. Turley recently completed the artwork for a children's picture book called *Wooo!*, using a combination of printmaking techniques and Photoshop. *Wooo!* is due to be published by Random House's David Fickling Books in 2013. Among many types of recognition, his work was selected for the Bologna Children's Book Fair Illustrators Exhibition in 2012.

Perler for svin [1,4]
Author/Illustrator Helene Uri/Ragnar Aalbu
First Published 2006, Mangschou, Norway
Original Language Norwegian

Ville veier [2]
Author/Illustrator Ragnar Aalbu
First Published 2010, Cappelen Damm, Norway
Original Language Norwegian

Harry og Roger får en slags venn [3]
Author/Illustrator Ragnar Aalbu
First Published 2011, Cappelen Damm, Norway
Original Language Norwegian

Harry og Roger på tur [5]
Author/Illustrator Ragnar Aalbu
First Published 2009, Cappelen Damm, Norway
Original Language Norwegian

Harry og Roger [6]
Author/Illustrator Ragnar Aalbu
First Published 2007, J.W. Cappelen Damm, Norway
Original Language Norwegian

ragnar aalbu

Ragnar Aalbu is a Norwegian illustrator and author of children's books, working with both traditional painting and drawing techniques as well as digital painting programs. His work is characterized by his use of folk references and funny characters in a graphic, collage-based manner. He has received various awards recognizing his art, including the Norwegian Ministry of Culture's award for books for kids and young adults. A graduate of the National Academy of Craft and Art, Aalbu currently resides in Oslo, where he runs an office for illustration called Estes / Aalbu together with fellow author-illustrator Max Estes.

Il più grande fiore del mondo
Author/Illustrator Jose Saramago/Emiliano Ponzi
First Published 2011, Feltrinelli, Italy
Original Language Italian

emiliano ponzi

Based in Milan, Emiliano Ponzi's bold textured illustration, a judicious use of line, and strong graphic compositions are perfect to express ideas for advertisements, magazines, books, newspapers, and animations. With worldwide clients such as the *New York Times*, *Time*, the *Economist*, and Saatchi & Saatchi New York, Emiliano has received numerous honors including the coveted Young Guns Award from the Art Directors Club. Ponzi's recently illustrated *Il più grande fiore del mondo (The Biggest Flower in the World)* is the only children's book written by Portuguese Nobel Laureate novelist José Saramago. The fascinating bildungsroman story was published by Feltrinelli Kids in December 2011.

2

4

3

Matilde Rosa Araújo – Um olhar de menina [1,4]
Author/Illustrator Adélia Carvalho/Marta Madureira
First Published 2010, Trinta Por Uma Linha, Portugal
Original Language Portuguese

I Ate an Owl [2]
Author/Illustrator Carlos Nogueira/Marta Madureira
First Published 2011, Tcharan, Portugal
Original Language Portuguese, English, Spanish

A crocodila mandona [3]
Author/Illustrator Adélia Carvalho/Marta Madureira
First Published 2010, Tcharan, Portugal
Original Language Portuguese

marta madureira

Portuguese designer, illustrator, and teacher Marta Madureira was born in Porto in 1977. She received her education at the fine arts faculty of the University of Porto and has illustrated numerous books for children that have earned her several awards – including the Naples Biennial Award in 2005 and the António de Almeida Prize in 2007. Among her extensive list of imaginative books made in collaboration with talented authors, Madureira has illustrated *As letras de números vestidas* (Trampolim, 2010), with text by João Pedro Mésseder and *A crocodila mandona* (Tcharan, 2010), with text by Adélia Carvalho.

How To [1]
Author/Illustrator Julie Morstad
First Published 2012, Simply Read Books, Canada
Original Language English

When I Was Small [2]
Author/Illustrator Sara O'Leary/Julie Morstad
First Published 2011, Simply Read Books, Canada
Original Language English

Untitled (sketch for How To) [3]
Illustrator Julie Morstad
Unpublished 2012

julie morstad

Julie Morstad is an award-winning illustrator and artist living in Vancouver. She received her bachelor of fine arts from the Alberta College of Art and Design in 2004 and has since produced art for kids' books, CD and book covers, fabric, wallpaper, and two animated music videos. Clients of Morstad's include Anti-Records, Chronicle Books, Drawn and Quarterly, HarperCollins, Warner Bros. Music, Penguin, and more. Using pencil, gouache, and a bit of digital software, Morstad tells poignant visual stories of childhood in books such as *Milk Teeth* (Drawn and Quarterly, 2011) and *Singing Away the Dark* (Simply Read Books, 2011).

interview
kitty crowther
children's book author and illustrator

Belgium-based children's book author and all-round atmospheric genius Kitty Crowther loves to tell a tale or two. A recent recipient of the prestigious Astrid Lindgren Memorial Award – and plenty of other name prizes – for a weird and wonderful body of work spanning almost 20 years and 35 books populated by frightened frogs, species-diverse birthday parties (from whale to sand fly), a desperately polite little death, helpless messies, and a smattering of friendly giants, the self-confessed storyteller weaves myths, folk tales, and everyday subjects into eerie, otherworldly journeys of discovery that add a sprinkling of humorous, melancholic subversion to the world of children's literature. Richly atmospheric and often more than a little spooky, her expertly crafted and evocative stories explore the nooks and narratives between the realms – and delight in questioning the reality suggested by our adult senses.

WE ARE ALL BIASED IN OUR PERCEPTION, ESPECIALLY WHEN IT COMES TO OURSELVES. SO, IF WE ASKED A FRIEND TO DESCRIBE YOU, WHAT WOULD HE OR SHE HAVE TO SAY?

(Laughs.) I would have to ask them first! Probably: honest, generous, a bit mysterious, and wise – well, that is what my friends would say! Maybe disturbing? It is a really interesting thought, because most of the time you meet people who are mirrors of yourself. I, for one, like to surround myself with people and stories that are as real as possible. You have to distinguish between real and fake, between what is genuine and what is constructed. Over time, many people build up faux characters. In contrast, I try to stay close to my heart in everyday life.

ANY EXCITING REAL-LIFE ADVENTURES THAT HAVE MADE YOU WHO YOU ARE?

When I was one year old, my father had this brilliant idea of buying a holiday home on the Dutch coast, next to a giant church and close to nature. At the time, we did not have a lot of money and it was a very simple house. We could just about afford the place and had very few things to fill it – but I always loved this very simple way of living. Some furniture had been left in the house, other stuff we found or managed to scrounge from somewhere else. I like objects to have a history and be part of life.

Other aspects that really shaped me: I have a hearing problem and I need to wear hearing aids. When something like that happens, it is up to you to choose if it is going to be easy or difficult. You simply have to deal with it. When I was little, it was a huge struggle to talk and write – and now here I am, doing books! At the same time, my disability gives me a kind of no man's land in my own mind; a place I can withdraw to when I want to block out the world and write. Your other senses have to take over. So, looking and watching have become very, very important to me – the sense of seeing more than what is on the surface has slipped into my way of thinking and working.

More often than not, it is so weird and fascinating when you see people who know how to talk and write extremely well ... but then you realize they have nothing to say! For me, it is the opposite: I have so much to say, but I don't know really how to say it. In a way, it is like spending a long time looking at people and saying, "how does it work, where are we going, what is this whole thing all about? What is it about love, feeling, and being together?" I had to find a way to understand it all. Also being half-Swedish, half-English and living in Belgium, I keep wondering, "Who the hell am I?" You have to ask yourself these questions to stay open and keep life interesting!

From my childhood, I have retained this huge capacity for amazement. To be touched by things and let things touch you. Birds, insects, flowers. It is funny because most of the time, we do not recognize the magic all around us anymore. We should constantly be shouting, "Look at this tree, look at this light!" And not care about what others might think.

CONSIDERING THIS SENSE OF AMAZEMENT AND EVERYDAY INFLUENCES, WHAT COMES FIRST WHEN YOU WRITE A NEW BOOK: NARRATIVE OR IMAGERY, SPECIFIC STYLES OR YOUR STORY'S PROTAGONISTS?

Looking back on about 17 or 18 years of doing books, I would have to say that it is always different. But I have read so much and looked at so much and been very moved by so many things that continue to live on inside me that they invariably swell up to the point where it all becomes a bit too much – and then I have to give it all back somehow. To use a different analogy: some people are

great cooks or mathematic geniuses or handy at repairing cars, and when you get this talent you need to share it and give something back.

What touches me most, though, are people: their tact, old people, children. When you think about it, we all look so similar, but are so different underneath. Considering the sheer number of people on earth, this is truly amazing! So, very often my stories start with a particular character – I am like a filmmaker who picks the actors first. Some of the time, I choose a realistic character, one who sounds like he might exist, and let him or her encounter something that doesn't exist. This is something I find really fascinating, this question of what is real or not, what might exist in between. After all, there are so many different kinds of theories floating around at the moment, whether you talk to a physicist or a psychic. And when you know that color doesn't really exist and that all the colors are inside your mind, you start to ask yourself some really tough questions. I love the invisible world, I love what isn't there. I believe in many things of which I don't know whether they exist – I mean, aliens, ghosts, gods, mermaids – anything, you name it. I don't really care if I see it or don't see it!

Since the beginning of time, people would tell each other stories and they would be focused on what they felt and thought about – fear, being together, finding yourself. And sometimes, these stories come back, maybe in a different setting or with different characters, but they are always meant to help us understand life through simplification. I often think that when you look at artifacts, whether Inuit sculptures, old ceramics, or whatever, they contain traces of an intuitive collective memory – the memory of previous instances of humanity. People recognize these but they don't know why! This happens to me all the time. So, once I have picked my characters, or once the characters have picked me, I don't know the end of my story. Just like a child, I simply fill a notebook with pictures and stories and follow them on their journey; I just draw and write and draw and write.

It is like having very powerful poetry that really touches you – you know the meaning of the words, you can see the pictures, but when you put them both together, it takes you somewhere completely different, somewhere you have never been to before. In the end, I just want to tell a good story. I have no more ambitions than that. Stories can make you softer, more open, wiser, cleverer. I love that feeling when you lose yourself in the story and think – wow – I have been somewhere else!

SO, DO YOU TAKE A DIFFERENT APPROACH WHEN YOU ILLUSTRATE SOMEONE ELSE'S WORK? DOES IT FEEL STRANGE – OR A WELCOME CHANGE FROM THE ONE-WOMAN SHOW?

Actually, if I read the story and straight away have it playing out in my head, then I will agree to do it. After all, I could not do two to three of my own books a year – people don't realize how long these stories are with you before they finally come out. They are always there, bubbling away inside you, and you have to feed and nurture them, even when they are not going anywhere. I am not so sure that I could come up with four great ideas every year, so sometimes it is good to go outside and see someone else's work. It is good to explore different shores, to cross borders, so to speak; they force you to draw things that you would not normally do. For example, my own stories tend to have forest and water, and then some more forest and water. It is fun when other people's stories put you in uncomfortable places, occasionally – I really like to surprise myself. But I still think that my own stories are the more powerful.

I AM LIKE A FILMMAKER WHO PICKS THE ACTORS FIRST.

BUT HOW DO YOU FILL THE SPACES BETWEEN CONCRETE TASKS, BOOKS OR STORIES? WHAT HAPPENS IN BETWEEN? WHAT COMES OUT OF YOUR PEN WHEN YOU DOODLE, WHEN THERE IS NO SPECIFIC TASK IN MIND?

I believe very strongly that when you draw and do it for a specific story, it instantly becomes charged with meaning. For example, when you create something to be placed in a shamanic bowl, something to fuel a ritual, you know that it is going to be used for a specific purpose and your work will be defined by that. So, when I know for whom and what I am drawing, the result is automatically quite a bit stronger because there is a goal and focus involved.

When I am actually doodling, what comes out of my pen is invariably a flood of characters – it is always people and usually quite strange ones at that. What really interests me is the point where strangeness and ugliness become beautiful. And that really comes out in my doodling. But generally speaking, it really helps to have an outside task or purpose. When you do things for yourself or on the side, you often do not care enough. I think that you have to care, and very strongly at that. I, for example, put more care into things that I do for other people. I simply find it more interesting to give than to receive. But after traveling so much and meeting so many people over the last year or so, my biggest luxury would be to give myself time and a small, defined exercise – just for the pleasure of working with pen and paper again. It would be like a little treat.

LET'S SAY YOU HAD TO SPIN A NEW STORY RIGHT NOW. OFF THE TOP OF YOUR HEAD, WHAT WOULD IT BE ABOUT?

Well, I love it when people are simply themselves and not shaped by the trappings and expectations of society too much. It is really fascinating and refreshing to see someone being themselves! And that is what makes life so incredibly rich. So, right now I have this character who is taking up more and more space in my mind. She is an older woman with very, very, very long hair and she comes across as quite frightening, really. In a way, she looks a little bit like a witch, but without all the obvious paraphernalia like a big broom or hat. Her incredibly long hair, however, is alive and can do things by itself. And this scary person has a daughter who is absolutely normal. I love looking at all these odd people in the streets or in the market, and sometimes I find that these daunting creatures are accompanied by little children. So, I wonder: How will the girl grow up with this strange, imposing person? What is their relationship?

IN MY OWN DRAWINGS I LIKE TO STATE: THIS EXISTS!

At the same time, this fleeting idea of a story tackles the general question of the space old – or lonely and disabled – people have in our modern, media-dominated technological world. Do we notice them? Do we talk about them? Why do we find them so strange and scary? In Japan, for example, people are totally used to being around old people and their bodies because everyone goes to public bath houses. Being old is a lot more visible over there, and this normalcy helps you get used to the idea of getting old yourself. In my own drawings I like to state: This exists! Even if it is something we do not quite understand. My job in life is to make it all visible: life, love, loneliness or friendship. Things are never as obvious or square as we think – it is my job to unsquare ideas!

YOU SEEM QUITE UNAFRAID OF TACKLING "BIG" OR UNCOMFORTABLE SUBJECTS. DO CHILDREN PERCEIVE THESE IN A WAY THAT IS DIFFERENT FROM OUR ADULT PERSPECTIVE? ARE THERE ANY LIMITS TO WHAT YOU WOULD TALK OR WRITE ABOUT?

I think as a child I was very, very scared of night and darkness. Totally terrified. And these thoughts and emotions take up a lot of space in your head. I was incredibly aware that there was something like life and death. I thought it was pretty amazing to wake up in the morning and still be alive! I was a very sensitive child, maybe too sensitive for my own good and with a great capacity for feeling. Luckily, my father was always willing to explain things to me, while my mother would rather say, "When you are older, we will tell you everything" – and then it never actually happened. Explaining helped me a lot, so I have a huge respect for people who will talk to children in the most honest possible way. I just love to have discussions with children when their heads are not yet filled with preconceptions or adult-conceived notions of the way you are "supposed to" talk and feel. They just need as much listening, interest, and input as possible. I believe that you should let the children pick their own direction in thought and emotions. They might come up with their own weird answers on death, belief, friendship, etc., but the result is going to be amazing and beautiful. Children are great because they sometimes see and notice things that we simply cannot perceive. Small kids are amazingly perceptive and quick; it is like they immediately grasp the entire picture and not just the small details we tend to home in on when we try to understand and dissect a situation. And if things are so huge, why put everything into small, neat boxes? Unfortunately, we often don't give children enough confidence to develop their own way of thinking.

With this in mind, I do not determine the morals or themes of my stories. Instead, I let my characters roam. While they might feature God talking to a little man, the respective story would not be about religion. I just loved the idea of what these protagonists might say to each other! In my stories, anything can talk – and anything can be talked about. So, when it comes to difficult subjects, nothing is really taboo at all. It just depends on how you introduce it into the story – it should be honest and heartfelt, not "look at how disturbing or clever I am!" In this spirit, I only tackle subjects I feel very strongly about and that I can deal with myself, not something that I do not understand. As long as you have a huge respect for children and always tell the truth, you should be okay. Within this framework, you can still pick your own approach. So, if you want to spin a yarn about where babies come from, you can still be very poetic, imaginative, or realistic!

La Visite de Petite Mort (all images)
Author/Illustrator Kitty Crowther
First Published 2004, Pastel, Belgium
Original Language France

CONSIDERING HOW STRONGLY YOU FEEL ABOUT YOUR OWN CREATIONS, HAVE YOU EVER GOTTEN INTO AN ARGUMENT WITH A PUBLISHER? IF SO, WHAT ABOUT?

When you do a book, you never do it totally on your own – you do it together with a publisher. And your publisher is a little bit like a mirror. Sometimes, when you encounter an obstacle or you find yourself in doubt, he or she will be there to help you find the right solution. On the other hand, you are also bound to argue about details. For example, you might think that the cover should be a different color, but they will say, "No, it is part of a collection and has to stay this way." Then you might get into an argument, but in the end you will have to let it go. Does the publisher always have the last say? Certainly not! It is all about navigation: Sometimes you have to weave your way through a storm, sometimes big waves, sometimes the weather is fine and clear ... you simply have to pick your battles. Or make the publisher think he or she came up with the idea in the first place! At the end of the day, this is your book, but you should do it together and not be too egocentric. But when I feel that what we argue about boils down to no more than an attitude or relationship problem and that it is not about the book itself, I can get a little bit angry.

Really big problems tend to surface early in the process – and sometimes it is better to step on the breaks and stop it all if you really do not like the way it is going. But when you are young and not famous (yet), it can be very difficult to know when to put your foot down and veto a project or development. In the end, your publisher should be someone you can trust.

DO YOU OCCASIONALLY FEEL STIFLED BY YOUR CURRENT SUCCESS AND THE ALMA-RELATED PUBLICITY?

No, the interesting thing is that it made many people turn around and think, "Hang on, this person received all this money for a body of work that is not simple or straightforward, but rather a little weird and uncomfortable." It helped to open up people's minds to more unusual thoughts, paths, and ideas! At the same time, it gave me more power and a form of strength – winning vindicates your choices, it tells you, "I wasn't wrong after all!"

LOOKING BACK – ANY REGRETS? ANYTHING YOU WOULD HAVE DONE DIFFERENTLY?

(Giggles.) I am laughing because it really boils down to how you decide to live your life. I will never have any regrets, ever. I view my books like a mother sees her children. Some are weaker and some are stronger, but I love them all the same.

WITH THIS IN MIND, WHAT WOULD YOU BE DOING IF YOU DECIDED TO ABANDON IT ALL (AND MONEY WAS NO OBJECT)?

I think I would write? No, that would still be the same thing as doing books. I would probably get involved with something to do with nature. I would study insects, birds, and flowers and build nature reserves. I am also very interested in ethnology and anthropology, in the way tribes and people get organized and interact. How people tick in all those different societies. When you see how different people are and what they believe in, it is all so fascinating. There is so much interesting stuff out there: distant healing, kinesiology, etc. And I would probably make ceramics: I would make a bowl and regale it with all my stories. And then I would probably do a book about it all!

* * *

Ab in den Wald
Author/Illustrator Maren Amini
Unpublished 2012
Original Language German

maren amini

Hamburg-based illustrator Maren Amini draws comics, comic-inspired illustrations, animations, diagrams, manuals, and anatomy drawings a million times more beautiful than one typically sees in a textbook. Her commercial editorial clients include *Financial Times Deutschland*, *Strapazin*, *Psychologie Heute*, and *HD Entertainment*. In May 2011, Amini was awarded the MDM grand prize for Children's Media for *Die Berglinge*, a children's TV animation series concept. Her first book for children is titled *Ab in den Wald*, about a slightly scary walk through the forest, which she wrote and illustrated herself.

Jorinde and Joringel (left page)
Author/Illustrator Brothers Grimm/Rilla Alexander
Unpublished 2012
Original Language English

Her Idea (right page)
Author/Illustrator Rilla Alexander
First Published 2011, Victionary, Hong Kong
Original Language English

rilla alexander

An Australian-born, Berlin-based designer, illustrator, and storyteller, Rilla Alexander is drawn to the simplest things in life – which are expressed beautifully in her artwork. The animal creatures she has invented dance across the Prado Museum's ceramics and stationery products, populate Swiss credit cards for Cornèr Bank, and sleep on the walls of the Hotel Fox in Copenhagen. As a member of Australian art and design collective Rinzen, she has published several books exploring the creative process. Alexander's all-ages picture book *Her Idea*, inspired by the classic Dr. Seuss book *Oh, the Places You'll Go!*, was launched in December 2010 with an exhibition at Colette in Paris.

Lily Loves [1,2]
Author/Illustrator Kai Lüftner/Judith Drews
First Published 2012, Simply Read Books, Canada
Original Language German

1

2

3

Traurig sein [3]
Author/Illustrator Kai Lüftner/Judith Drews
Unpublished 2012
Original Language German

Berlin Wimmelbuch [4]
Author/Illustrator Judith Drews
First Published 2011, Wimmelbuchverlag, Germany
Original Language German

judith drews

Judith Drews is a Berlin-based illustrator and designer with a wide variety of clients in the illustration industry – publishing houses, magazines, newspapers, fashion labels, advertizing agencies, and design companies. Her illustration work is for both children and adults, and as a long-time lover of kids' books, Drews has created over 10 highly acclaimed books for young people in collaboration with various authors. Drews's illustrations have been published, exhibited, or reviewed in Germany, United Kingdom, United States, Canada, Taiwan, France, Spain, Italy, Switzerland, and Costa Rica. In 2010, she was nominated for the German Design Award.

SHOP
TV VIDEOS
ALEX
NO.8
2255
Paule
Eis
OFFEN
BUCHSEGELN
LESUNG mit CALLY
KIEZ TIPP
Paule
3,-
hmmm
WERTVOLL

Little Pink [1]
Illustrator Stina Wirsén
Personal Work 2012, Sweden

stina wirsén

One of Sweden's most highly regarded illustrators, Stina Wirsén was born in Stockholm, where she lives and works today. Finishing at Stockholm's Konstfack University College of Arts, Craft and Design in 1992, Wirsén is the author of over 40 books for children, many of them co-authored by her mother, Carin Wirsén. Together with product designer Anna Hörling, Wirsén created the Brokiga brand, a collection of quality products for children. With Brokiga, the beloved family of characters often found in her children's books comes to life on a variety of household products. In addition to her wildly popular creations for very young children, Wirsén works with a wide variety of commercial clients.

3

2

Where's Little Pink and All the Brokiga Little Friends? [2]
Author/Illustrator Carin Wirsén/Stina Wirsén
First Published 2007, Bonnier Carlsen, Sweden
Original Language Swedish

Gul! [3,4]
Author/Illustrator Stina Wirsén
First Published 2012, Bonnier Carlsen, Sweden
Original Language Swedish

4

Il Était plusieurs fois une forêt [1]
Author/Illustrator Elisa Géhin
First Published 2009, Éditions Thierry Magnier, France
Original Language French

1

2

Lunon chamboule tout [2]
Author/Illustrator Agnès Bertron-Martin/Elisa Géhin
First Published 2010, Éditions Benjamins Media, France
Original Language French

Des pieds et des mains [3]
Author/Illustrator Collectif/Elisa Géhin
First Published 2011, Milan Jeunesse, France
Original Language French

elisa géhin

Elisa Géhin's most popular kids' book, *Le Doudou qui parle (The Blanket that Speaks)* is the endearing story of a little girl who cannot sleep and finds herself in a conversation with her favorite stuffed animal. *Le Doudou qui parle* was written by Frédéric Kessler and published by Thierry Magnier in 2010, filled with page after page of Géhin's striking, simple, eye-catching illustrations that delight young children. Géhin was born in 1984 in the Vosges Mountains of France, and after passing through the École Estienne and then Strasbourg's School of Decorative Arts, she now lives and works in Paris.

Tonino l'invisibile
Author/Illustrator Gianni Rodari/Alessandro Sanna
First Published 2009, Emme Edizioni, Italy
Original Language Italian

alessandro sanna

Born in Nogara, Italy in 1975, Alessandro Sanna lives and works today in the Italian province of Mantua. A graduate of the Institute of Design in Verona, he has authored and illustrated an extensive collection of books. In addition to his wide-ranging work for international publishing houses and advertising agencies, Sanna holds training courses for teachers on creativity and hosts workshops for painting and drawing in schools all over Italy. He also takes part in collective and solo exhibitions of his artistic work. In 2006, he received the Andersen Prize for "Best Art Book" with his title, *Hai Mai Visto Mondrian?*, published by the Italian publisher Artebambini.

1

2

3

Bibbi og katten [1,2]
Author/Illustrator Gry Moursund
First Published 2011, Cappelen Damm, Norway
Original Language Norwegian

Bukkene Bruse på badeland [3,4]
Author/Illustrator Bjørn F. Rørvik/Gry Moursund
First Published 2009, Cappelen Damm, Norway
Original Language Norwegian

gry moursund

Gry Moursund's first picture book *Himmelkua* (The Heavenly Cow) was published in 1999. Since then, she has illustrated more than 20 children's books. Moursund, who was born in 1969 in the north of Norway, was awarded the 2001 Norwegian Culture Ministry's prize for "Best Picture Book of the Year," for her book *Arkimedes og Brødskiva (Archimedes and the Slice of Bread)*. Other awards include the Brage Prize in 2003 and two gold medals and four silver medals for Norway's The Most Beautiful Books of the Year Award. Moursund was educated at the National Academy of Craft and Art in Oslo, as well as at the Royal College of Arts in London, and currently lives in Berlin.

DUSJ

I am Aan [1]
Author/Illustrator Christopher Corr
First Published 2011, Katha, India
Original Language English, Hindi

The Goggle-Eyed Goats [2]
Author/Illustrator Stephen Davies/Christopher Corr
First Published 2012, Andersen Press, United Kingdom
Original Language English

Children's Picture Atlas [3]
Illustrator Christopher Corr
First Published 2012, Weldon Owen, Australia
Original Language English

christopher corr

Illustrator Christopher Corr was born in London and studied at the Royal College of Art. His round-the-world travels provide much inspiration for his work – which ranges from book jackets, posters, advertisements, a World AIDS Day campaign, to dozens of children's books. Corr works with gouaches on hand made Italian or Indian paper, creating new stories with celebrated authors, as well as new takes on classic stories. One such popular collection was Corr's newly illustrated anthology of Rudyard Kipling's classic *Just So Stories* (Candlewick Press, 2004), made accessible for both younger and older children to enjoy.

Red Octopus [4]
Illustrator Christopher Corr
Personal Work 2010

Salon de l'Illustration
& de Livre pour
l'Enfance &
la Jeunesse
Tome 2
11-12-13
Février
2011
Benjamin Chaud

Salon de l'illustration [1]
Illustrator Benjamin Chaud
Poster 2011, France

2

4

3

Untitled [2,3,4]
Illustrator Benjamin Chaud
Sketches 2012, France

benjamin chaud

Benjamin Chaud, born in 1975 in a small village in the Hautes-Alpes of France, studied applied arts in Paris and later decorative arts in Strasbourg. After spending nine years in Marseille, he now works in Paris. Chaud has said he identifies himself most with the character Calvin in the classic comic strip *Calvin and Hobbes*, and indeed, his own illustrative work has moved more and more toward the comic. His lovable comic creatures appear in books from Actes Sud, Nathan, Bayard, and many other publishers. Recent bestsellers illustrated by Chaud include *Une chanson d'ours* (Édition Hélium, 2011) and *Adieu Chausette* (Édition Hélium, 2010).

La Baleine du ciel [1]
Illustrator Nicolas Gouny
Illustration 2010, France

L'Arbre aux bonbons [2]
Illustrator Nicolas Gouny
Personal Work 2009

Le Petit Homme triste de la lune [3]
Illustrator Nicolas Gouny
Illustration 2010, France

nicolas gouny

After spending 10 years in educational publishing, Nicolas Gouny has been living in the center of France since 2008 to devote himself full time to illustrations for children. In a duo called La Parenthèse Enchantée, Gouny and his partner Delphine create jewelry and other objects based on his illustrations. Gouny's books, numbering over 10, are originally published in French, but have been translated into several languages. The fantasy world he imagines and draws in his books, like the recent *L'oiseau fait son nid ... moi aussi!* (Scarabea, 2011), is one filled with fairies and monsters, lovers, giraffes, children, trees, and sunsets.

Nuit de rêve [1,2]
Author/Illustrator Laurent Moreau
First Published 2012, Actes Sud, France
Original Language French

À quoi penses-tu? [4]
Author/Illustrator Laurent Moreau
First Published 2011, Édition Helium, France
Original Language French

laurent moreau

French illustrator Laurent Moreau was born in the United Kingdom in 1982. Now living is Strasbourg, Moreau is the author of several children's books and is involved in the entire production process from text to artwork to printing. The multi-talented illustrator also does graphic design work for newspapers and cultural programs, and dabbles in photography, especially using Polaroid film. In February 2012, his most recent book came out, entitled *Nuit de rêve*. The bedtime book is published by French children's press Actes Sud Junior and features 32 pages of beautiful stand-alone graphic illustrations.

Untitled [3]
Illustrator Laurent Moreau
Sketchbook 2012
Original Language French

REX
BYE

Knight Night [1,2,4]
Author/Illustrator Owen Davey
First Published 2011, Templar Publishing, United Kingdom
Original Language English

Foxly's Feast [3,5]
Author/Illustrator Owen Davey
First Published 2010, Templar Publishing, United Kingdom
Original Language English

owen davey

Owen Davey has had his illustrations published on every continent except Antarctica. A freelance illustrator living and working in Bristol, United Kingdom, some of Davey's commercial clients include Orange, BBC, Microsoft, Persil, the *Guardian*, the *New York Times*, the *Telegraph*, and Jamie Oliver. Davey won the 2011 Junior Magazine Most Promising New Talent Award for his debut picture book, *Foxly's Feast*. This witty, wordless picture book, which was also highly commended by the 2009 Macmillan Children's Book Prize, is the story of a hungry fox named Foxly as he decides which animal to eat for his next meal. Foxly eyes up the chickens, the ducks, the fish, and the rabbits, ultimately coming to an unexpected conclusion.

Along a Long Road
Author/Illustrator Frank Viva
First Published 2011, Little, Brown Books for Young Readers, United States
Original Language English
Editor: Susan Rich

frank viva

Frank Viva is an illustrator and graphic designer who has won more than 300 awards working with tiny non profits, big corporations, and everything in between. His illustrations have appeared in publications such as *Time*, *Esquire*, the *New York Times*, the *Boston Globe*, and on the cover of the *New Yorker*, in addition to two recent books for children. The multi-talented artist's first children's book, *Along a Long Road*, was released by Little Brown in 2011, and his second, *A Trip to the Bottom of the World with Mouse*, appeared in 2012 from Random House. Both books are exciting stories about travel and adventure.

a bridge

Along a long road

This Is Silly
Author/Illustrator Gary Taxali
First Published 2010, Scholastic Press, United States
Original Language English

gary taxali

Gary Taxali is an award-winning illustrator whose work has appeared in many major magazines. He has exhibited in galleries and museums throughout North America and Europe, and has even launched his own toy company, Chump Toys. He is a founding member of the Illustrators' Partnership of America and sits on the advisory board of *3×3: The Magazine of Contemporary Illustration* and the Stamp Advisory Committee of Canada Post. In 2011, Taxali released his first children's book, entitled *This Is Silly!* and published by Scholastic Press. Steve Heller writes of Taxali: "His style, inspired by vintage comics and advertising art, is repurposed with the goal of communicating the ironies and comical essence of popular culture."

hee.
Tumbling tomfoolery!

There goes
MANiC MONKEY,

Ho-ho, ha-ha, yuk-yuk, tee-hee,

1

2

3

Il grande Alfredo [1,3]
Author/Illustrator Daniele Melani
First Published 2010, Orecchio Acerbo, Italy
Original Language Italian

Lola [2,4,5]
Author/Illustrator Daniele Melani
First Published 2011, Orecchio Acerbo, Italy
Original Language Italian

daniele melani

Daniele Melani's artistic spirit is fueled by family, art, and motorcycle rides – he is always seeking the new and challenging the status quo. His art is imbued with energy, joy, and tawdriness in works that are huge, tiny, delicate, splattered, textured, collaged, stenciled, typographic. His work is exhibited at Gallery L'Affiche in Milan, Italy, and is widely collected around the world. Milani, who has been profiled in *3x3, The Magazine of Illustration*, is represented by Piccioli Illustration in Italy and Morgan Gaynin Inc. in New York. He lives in Italy with fellow artist Simona Mulazzani and their daughter.

HAAH

1

2

4

3

Jabberwock [1,2,3]
Author/Illustrator Raphael Urwiller
First Published 2010, Icinori, France
Original Language English

Momotaro [4,5]
Author/Illustrator Raphael Urwiller & Mayumi Otero
First Published 2012, Icinori, France
Original Language French

raphael urwiller

Raphael Urwiller is one half of a small, independent publishing house called Icinori. Along with fellow illustrator Mayumi Otero, they produce gorgeous little limited edition hand-printed, hand-cut prints and books. Using a two- or three-color process, Urwiller's work usually consists of perfectly simple drawings, overlaid colors, and patches of vibrant layered patterns. Two of his well-crafted books tell the classic tales of Jason and the Argonauts from Greek mythology and Lewis Carroll's beloved poem "Jabberwocky." Urwiller's commercial clients include the European Council, *Tiger Magazine*, and *Forbes* Asia.

x, tout est doux,
x - Le vois-tu ? -
s feuilles.

Dans la forêt du paresseux [1]
Author/Illustrator Sophie Strady/Anouck Boisrobert & Louis Rigaud
First Published 2011, Édition Hélium, France
Original Language French

Popville [2,3]
Author/Illustrator Joy Sorman/Anouck Boisrobert & Louis Rigaud
First Published 2009, Édition Hélium, France
Original Language French

2

3

4

Tip tap, mon imagier interactif [4]
Author/Illustrator Anouck Boisrobert & Louis Rigaud
First Published 2011, Édition Hélium, France
Original Language French

louis rigaud

A graduate of the School of Decorative Arts of Strasbourg, Louis Rigaud works as a freelancer in multimedia creation and illustration. He is truly a multi-talented artist, working in print, moving images, Web design, and video games. Much of Rigaud's work has an educational dimension, transmitting knowledge to kids in the form of children's books and to adults through popular science and cultural projects. A recent project called *Tip tap* was released by Hélium in 2012. *Tip tap* is a picture book with illustrations for over 200 words, including landscape terms and means of transport. An interactive CD is included with the book to provide a complete learning experience for young children.

Otto rijdt heen en weer naar de stad [1]
Author/Illustrator Tom Shamp
First Published 2011, Lannoo, Belgium
Original Language Dutch

Untitled [2]
Illustrator Tom Shamp
Biscuits Box 2004, Philip's Biscuits, Belgium

Untitled [3]
Illustrator Tom Shamp
Exhibition Poster Compilation of nature elements from the picture book *Le Fabuleux Amour d'Aucassin et Nicolette* (2010, Albin Michel, France) and city elements from various picture books made over the years.

tom schamp

Tom Schamp was born in Mortsel, Belgium, and grew up in Brussels. After graduating from Sint-Lukas Brussels University College of Art and Design, he studied graphic arts in Poznan, Poland, where he got the opportunity to experiment with various new style elements. He gradually developed a style of his own, using acrylic paint on cardboard. Schamp's illustrations appeal to adults and children alike. His assignments come from an international mix of customers, including renowned children's books publishers (Albin Michel, Milan, Lannoo), magazines *(Humo, Playboy)*, newspapers *(De Morgen, De Standaard, NRC Handelsblad)*, and various advertising agencies.

www.tomschamp.com
Coala
Fame
Warhol Soup
I ♥ NY
UNIVERSITY
OFF
HOTEL
California
Broadway
ART
BIG
BIG
BIG
BUSINESS
SOAP
SOAP
SOAP
METERS
ARCHIV
ARCHIV
CITY
TWIN
TOWERS
EURO
MARTINI
DANSK
Bottle
Neg
VINO
SCHOOL
NIGHT
& DAY
BROAD
CAST
TOURBUS
BOUTIQUE
BB
FULLYBOOKED
culture
nature

OTTO-KAR
B R E A K
F A S T
B U S
vrac
I
N
HOT
DOG
Club Trop
Tom
CHAMP
USA
DEPANINI & CO.
24/24
FRUIT
RE PAS SAGE
OTTOSTOP
M
M&S
TAXI
VERT
TAXI
BLEU
CAB
TOSTADOS
UNIDOS
OTTO
25
PRIOR
LAPOSTE
JOHN
REINDEER
MAS
Otto
in de
Stad
RADIO
SCHAMP
Ham
Burger
KING'S
Schilders
Schamp & zoon

Otto's Cars
Illustrator Tom Shamp
Illustration Compilation of the vehicles appearing in the picture book series *Otto rijdt heen en weer – Otto in de stad – Otto in de sneeuw* (2007–2012, Lannoo, Belgium).

Aoki [1,3,4]
Author/Illustrator Annelore Parot
First Published 2010, Milan, France
Original Language French

Yumi [2]
Author/Illustrator Annelore Parot
First Published 2009, Milan, France
Original Language French

annelore parot

Though Annelore Parot is a current resident of France, it is evident in her gorgeously illustrated picture books that she is a world traveler. In her popular *Kokeshi* series published by Chronicle Books, Parot manages to incorporate aspects of Japanese language and culture in a fun and educational way for children living anywhere. Furthermore, the books in the series are made surprisingly interactive with sneak-peek flaps, fun die-cuts, and lavish gatefolds. Each book is an experience that takes young readers into a world of cherry blossom trees, high-speed trains, and Zen gardens. As one might guess from her mastery of intricate patterns, Parot also designs textiles and household items.

KO
Kə
Shi

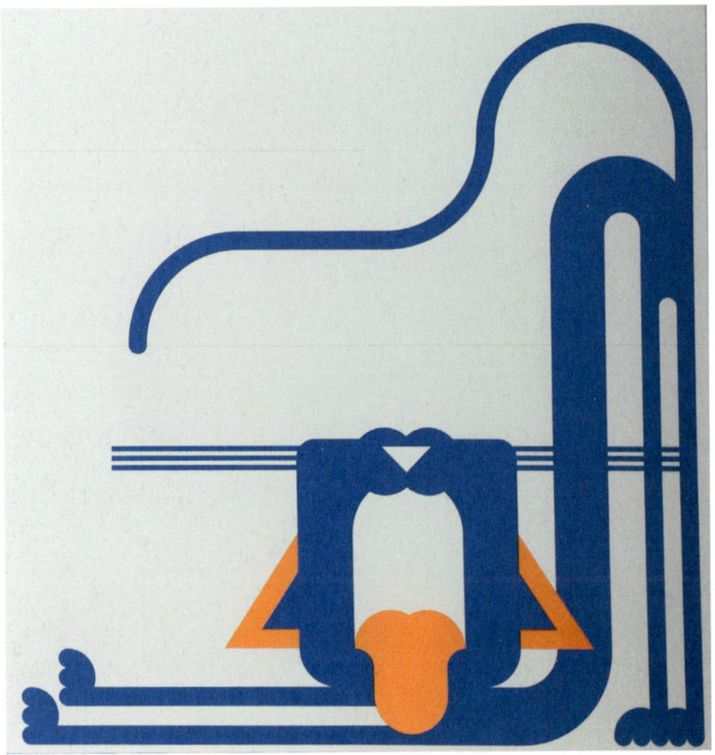

Quatro gatos, negro flacos (left page)
Author/Illustrator Didi Grau/Christian Montenegro
First Published 2010, El Gato Con Bote, Argentina
Original Language Spanish

Peleonas Mentirosas y Haraganas (right page)
Author/Illustrator Didi Grau/Christian Montenegro
First Published 2009, Argentina
Original Language Spanish

christian montenegro

Argentinean illustrator Christian Montenegro first studied comics in Alberto Breccia's atelier, and later studied graphic design at Buenos Aires University. Since 2002, he works primarily in digital media, mixing concepts from the world of design with his experience making comics. He says his style could be compared to that of a Lego system: simple parts are combined piece by piece to ultimately create a complex and intricate system. His work has been published and exhibited in Argentina and around the world, including at the Bologna Children's Book Fair, the Figures-Futur exhibition in Paris, and at two Pictoplasma exhibitions.

?
¿Estáis todas saNas?
pregunta el conde de Rabana.

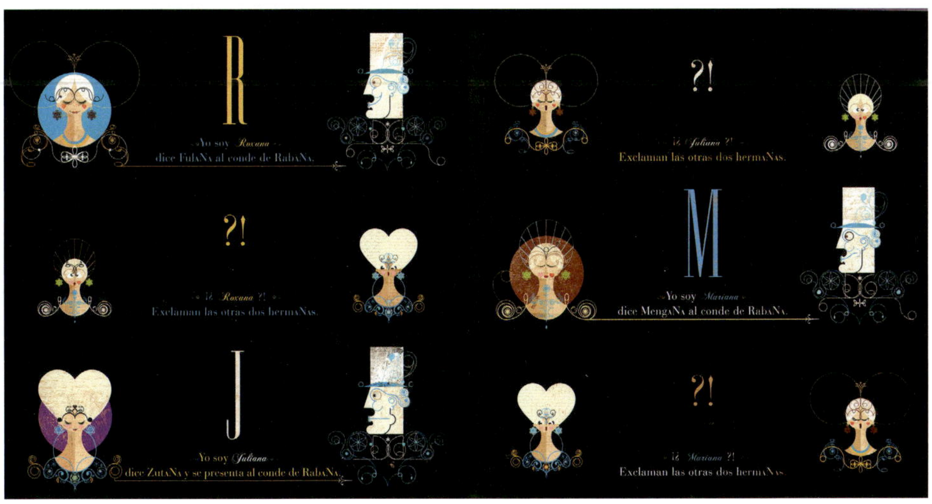
R
Yo soy Roxana
dice FulaNa al conde de RabaNa.
?!
¿Juliana?!
Exclaman las otras dos hermaNas.
?!
¿Roxana?!
Exclaman las otras dos hermaNas.
M
Yo soy Mariana
dice MengaNa al conde de RabaNa.
J
Yo soy Juliana
dice ZutaNa y se presenta al conde de RabaNa.
?!
¿Mariana?!
Exclaman las otras dos hermaNas.

MENGANA

Lady René (left page)
Author/Illustrator Harry S. Miller/Laura Varsky
First Published 2011, Pehuen, Chile
Original Language Spanish

Little Duckling (right page)
Author/Illustrator H. C. Andersen/Laura Varsky
First Published 2004, Gestalten, Germany
Original Language English

laura varsky

Laura Varsky is a graphic designer and illustrator from Buenos Aires, Argentina. Her first forays into the design world came through her involvement with the local independent rock scene. She gradually asserted herself as a designer, specializing in the design of books and CD sleeves. In 2006 she received a Latin Grammy as Art Director for best record packaging. Rediscovering the world of illustration, she began working for editorial projects, several labels, and artistic projects. After a 10-year professorship in Typography at the School of Design at the University of Buenos Aires, she continues coordinating workshops and giving lectures extensively throughout Latin America and Spain.

Esqueci-me como se chama
Author/Illustrator Daniil Kharms/Gonçalo Viana
First Published 2011, Bruaá Editora, Portugal
Original Language Portuguese

gonçalo viana

Illustration has always been Gonçalo Viana's first love. Born in Lisbon, he studied architecture before moving to London to work at an architecture practice — but eventually he returned to Lisbon to follow his passion and work as a freelance illustrator. However, geometry seeps back into his work, providing a frame for his smart concepts, bold colors, and textural landscapes. Viana aims to translate complex ideas into simple and engaging images. His conceptual approach has garnered recognition from *Communication Arts*, *3x3 Magazine*, and Lürzer's Archive's *200 Best Illustrators Worldwide*. In 2012 his work was selected for the prestigious Bologna Children's Book Fair Guest of Honour Country Exhibition.

The Memory Tree [1]
Author/Illustrator Britta Teckentrup
First Published 2012, Orchard Books (Hachette), United Kingdom

Not Out of the Woods Yet [2,3]
Author/Illustrator Britta Teckentrup
Personal Project

Animal ABC [4]
Illustrator Britta Teckentrup
Personal Project

britta teckentrup

The artist, writer, and illustrator Britta Teckentrup was born in Hamburg and raised in the town of Wuppertal, Germany. Teckentrup moved to London in 1988 to study illustration and art at Saint Martins College and the Royal College of Art. Now living in Berlin, she is the author and illustrator of many well-loved kids' books, including the best-selling *Big Smelly Bear*, *How Big Is the World*, and *Grumpy Cat*, which was selected by the Booktrust's Bookstart scheme, so 250,000 copies were distributed to families throughout the United Kingdom. Teckentrup's books number over 40 and have been published in over 20 countries, and her fine art is frequently exhibited at galleries and fairs around the world.

A
E
W
G
Q
K
G
B
B
O
M

PIAZZA FIUME
Il gallo che canta
Oggi

Il filobus numero 75 [1,3,4]
Author/Illustrator Gianni Rodari/Blanca Gómez
First Published 2012, Emme Edizioni, Italy
Original Language Italian

Léonard a une sensibilité de gauche [2]
Author/Illustrator Vincent Delerm/Blanca Gómez
First Published 2011, Actes Sud, France
Original Language French

blanca gómez

Blanca Gómez is a Madrid-based illustrator and designer. Her clients include *Monocle* and *Dwell* magazines, CNN Money, Honda, Velocity Art and Design, Orange, and Movistar. Gómez's most recent venture was illustrating a book for children written by popular kid's writer Gianni Rodari, which was published by the Italian publisher Edizioni El in 2012. The book, titled *Il filobus numero 75*, takes readers on a trip through Rome with the trolleybus number 75. On this special trip, the bus makes a turn – unexpectedly carrying all the passengers out of the city to spend a day in the forest enjoying the beauty of nature.

Do You Know What I Am?
Author/Illustrator Chad Geran
First Published 2011, Self-published, Canada
Original Language English

chad geran

While living in New Zealand in 2007, Canadian illustrator and art director Chad Geran began a self-initiated children's book project. He started posting the pages he created to a blog, which generated broad interest in his work. The project was recently relaunched, and two children's eBooks created by Geran are now available online for mac, iPhone, and iPad. The first book, *Do You Know What I Am?: A Rhyming Book*, is available free to make sure it gets into the hands of kids and illustration lovers around the world. After working in New Zealand from 2006 to 2007, Chad now makes his home in Regina, Canada with his wife and son.

I Like Vegetables
Author/Illustrator Lorena Siminovich
First Published 2010, Templar Publishing, United Kingdom
Original Language English

lorena siminovich

Originally from Buenos Aires, Lorena Siminovich is a San Francisco-based designer, artist, and author. Siminovich has written and illustrated over 20 books for children with Chronicle Books, Templar UK, and Candlewick Press. Her books have been published in seven different languages, garnered several awards, and received praise from *Parents Magazine*, *Kirkus Reviews*, the *Telegraph*, and the *Martha Stewart Show*, among many other media outlets. With a retro, modish feel, her illustrative work is incredibly popular with readers of any age. A creative force, she is also the founder of Petit Collage, a line of modern wall décor and accessories with a vintage twist.

1

Alphabet [1]
Author/Illustrator Marion Billet
Postcard 2006, Cartes d'Art, France

Transports [2]
Author/Illustrator Marion Billet
Poster 2007, L'Affiche Moderne, France

2

Cerf [3]
Author/Illustrator Marion Billet
Poster 2007, L'Affiche Moderne, France

marion billet

Children love Marion Billet's charming world of adorable and colorful animal characters. Billet has published over 80 books for children in 11 different countries, often in series of books that follow the same characters through different stories. Such series include the *Noodle* books, which take readers along on the adventures of a lovable panda, the *Chamalo* books, about a friendly tiger, and the *Paul et Félicie* series, about two young friends. Much of Billet's work has been published by the young independent publisher Nosy Crow, and her characters have appeared in magazines, on stationery, and even as toys. Billet was born in 1982 in Lyon, France.

ZzZ
marion

Papatineurs [1]
Author/Illustrator Marc Boutavant
First published 2004 Djeco, France
Original Language French

marc boutavant

Originally from Burgundy, Marc Boutavant now lives and works in Paris. His work springs from a wry observation of life and the interaction of his friends and children in order to imagine creatures who share adventures in his books like the popular *Around the World with Mook* (Chronicle Books, 2009). Light-hearted horror, comedy and pathos combine to form rich narratives that Boutavant often creates in collaboration with other authors. When not creating work for kids, Boutavant approaches his illustration projects for a wide variety of clients such as Marks & Spencer, The *New York Times*, Sony Music, and the *New Yorker* with similar energy.

Arbracadabra [2]
Author/Illustrator Marc Boutavant
First published 2004 Djeco, France
Original Language French

Multimouk [3]
Author/Illustrator Marc Boutavant
First published 2011, Millimages, France
Original Language French

RAINBOW
COOKIE
CUPCAKES

Petits Ruisseaux
Author/Illustrator Cathy Ytak/Vincent Mathy
First Published 2011, Sarbacane, France
Original Language French

vincent mathy

Born in Liège, Belgium, in 1971, Vincent Mathy is well known for his illustrative work. After studying at the St. Luc Institute in Brussels, he became passionate about visual communication in the broad sense of the term, especially about children's illustrations. He currently lives at the Belgian border between Liège and Maastricht, where he has created about 30 children's books, as well as posters, flyers, and drawings for magazine articles and advertisements. Whimsical, colorful, and retro-inspired, his images are slightly reminiscent of the late great illustrator Richard Scarry.

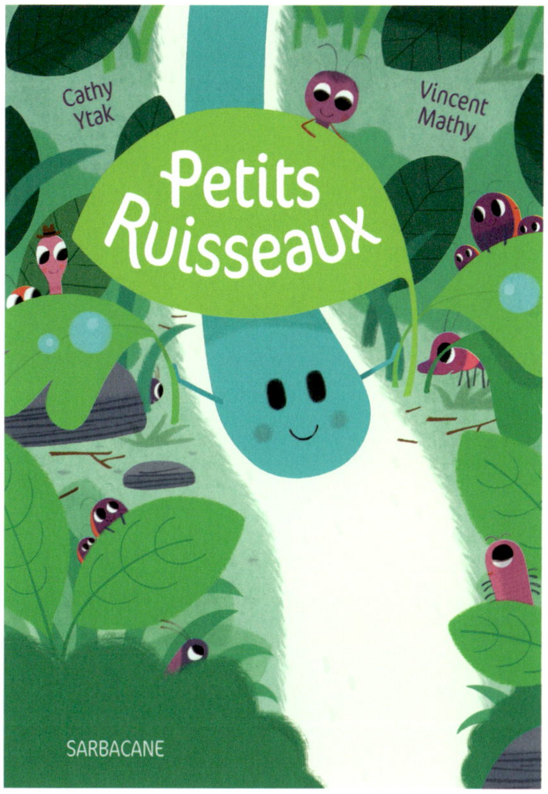
Cathy
Ytak
Vincent
Mathy
Petits
Ruisseaux
SARBACANE

2

3

4

5

A Bit Lost [1,3,4]
Author/Illustrator Chris Haughton
First Published 2009, Borim Press, Korea
Original Language Korean

Oh No, George! [2,5]
Author/Illustrator Chris Haughton
First Published 2012, Walker Books, United Kingdom
Original Language English

chris haughton

Chris Haughton is an Irish designer and illustrator who has been authoring and illustrating children's books since 2010. Children respond strongly to the brightly colored images that Haughton creates to portray likeable animal characters. His first book, *A Bit Lost* (Walker, 2010), is the story of an owl searching for its mother. It has been translated into 10 languages and has won eight awards in six countries, including the Dutch Picture Book of the Year. His most recent book, *Oh No, George!*, was released in March 2012. Before Haughton became involved with making books, he was active in fair trade, and he has been a supporter of and designer for the fair-trade company People Tree for many years.

Mokomaki [1,2,3]

Author/Illustrator Satu Kontinen

First Published 2011, WSOY, Finland

Original Language Finnish

1

4

Hupskeikkaa [4]
Author/Illustrator Satu Kontinen
First Published 2010, WSOY, Finland
Original Language Finnish

satu kontinen

Finnish graphic designer Satu Kontinen established a one-woman design firm called Satukala in 2001. Her clients include companies, nonprofits, governmental / municipal organizations, publishing houses, and event organizers. She is focusing on aesthetic graphic design that flows smoothly through all types of media. Graduating from Pekka Halosen Academy in Finland in 1999, Kontinen recently broadened her scope to include illustrations for children. She recently designed and illustrated a hilarious book about motherhood, *Vuoden Mutsi (Mom of the Year)* which was written by Katja Lahti and Satu Rämö.

Alba Blabla & moi
Author/Illustrator Alex Cousseau/Anne-Lise Boutin
First Published 2011, Éditions du Rouergue, France
Original Language French

anne-lise boutin

Born in 1977, Anne-Lise Boutin has been living and working in Paris since 1995. She attended the Paris school of art and design, École Duperré, in arts and textile prints, then the École of Arts Décoratifs. She has illustrated the children's books *Ogres et ogresses* (Éditions Hatier, 2006), *Dico des signes et symboles religieux* (2006, Actes Sud Junior), *Contes et mythes des Maasaïs* (Actes Sud Junior, 2007), and *L'Ami l'iguane* (Éditions du Rouergue, 2008). Boutin's illustrations are made by using pastels, cut paper, and numeric collages, and are inspired by popular arts, Mexican calaveras, the fantastic, and the bizarre.

Nove storie sull'amore
Author/Illustrator Giovanna Zoboli/Ana Ventura
First Published 2011, Topipittori, Italy
Original Language Italian

ana ventura

Ana Ventura is an artist and illustrator living in Lisbon. She graduated in painting from the University of Lisbon's Faculty of Fine Arts in 2000 with a major in engraving. Her work has been exhibited in solo and group shows since 1996 and is represented in private collections in Portugal and abroad. Ventura's work evocatively combines modern decorative and design elements with figures sometimes reminiscent of medieval Byzantine art. Ventura's first children's book, *Nove storie sull'amore*, tells nine tales about having compassion for one's fellow beings. The book has been published both in a special limited edition and in a trade edition, which has so far been translated into four languages.

Pampilio
Author/Illustrator Irena Tuwim/Monika Hanulak
First Published 2010, Wytwórnia, Poland
Original Language Polish

monika hanulak

Educated at the Academy of Fine Arts in Warsaw, where she now teaches, Monika Hanulak is an expert in book design and illustration. She has collaborated with various artists, writers, and publishers, and in 2004 she co-created an art group called CMYK. Winner of the Warsaw Graphic Award three different times, she has participated in many fine arts exhibitions as well. Her modest and clever illustrations appear in the children's book *Pampilio*, a fairytale about a land of animals and a mysterious tree. A collaboration between Hanulak and Irena Tuwim, the book has been rightfully described by critics as "ingenious" and "fresh."

1

2

3

4

Romance [1]
Author/Illustrator Bernard Granger
First Published 2013, Albin Michel Jeunesse, France
Original Language French

Bim de la jungle [2]
Author/Illustrator Bernard Granger
First Published 2004, Éditions Thierry Magnier, France
Original Language French

Mon ami ... rond [3]
Author/Illustrator Bernard Granger
First Published 2007, Albin Michel Jeunesse, France
Original Language French

5

L'Imagier des Gens (alternate versions) [4,5]
Author/Illustrator Bernard Granger
First Published 2008, Albin Michel Jeunesse, France
Original Language French

blex bolex

Born Bernard Granger in Douai, France, in 1966, Blexbolex studied printmaking at the School of Fine Arts in Angoulême before developing his highly stylized ligne claire illustration. Known for his willingness to experiment with illustration and printing techniques, the book illustrator and cartoonist has made a name for himself with his children's books and graphic novels for Thierry Magnier, Cornélius, and Pipifax, among others. In 2009, he received a prize for "Best Book Design From All Over the World" for his *L'Imagier des gens* (2008) at the Leipzig Book Fair. Of his simplified style, Blexbolex says: "I try to do simple things, to make them as well as I can, and that is difficult enough."

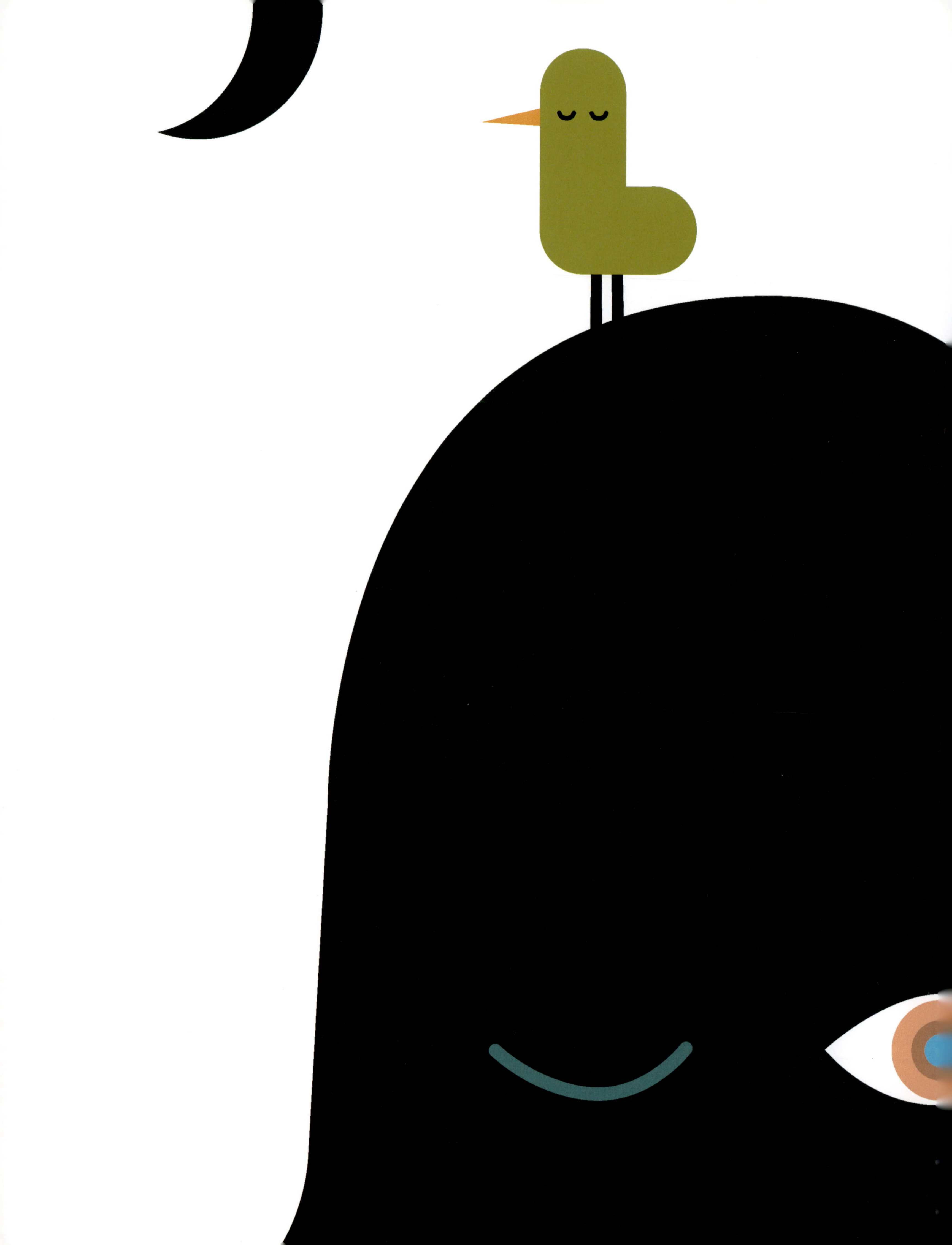

Le Yéti
Author/Illustrator Fabrice Houdry
First Published 2006, Thierry Magnier, France
Original Language French

fabrice houdry

In 2002, Fabrice Houdry created Yaralt and set up his studio as an illustrator in Rouen, France. As Yaralt, he worked with many clients such as Éditions Thierry Magnier, *WAD* magazine, *ExtraSmall*, and the Festival Bbmix. He was joined in 2005 by Pierre-Adrien Draco, photographer and director of a young publishing house, and in 2007 graphic and motion designer Ludovic Villain joined the team. Studio Yaralt, both a concept and a place, is currently a multidisciplinary studio and gallery space, creating and exhibiting a wide variety of illustrations, moving images, books, prints, and objects.

Y recuerda ...
Author/Illustrator Brothers Grimm/Juanjo G. Oller
First Published 2007, Milimbo, Spain
Original Language Spanish

juanjo g. oller

Juanjo Oller has been a designer and illustrator since 1998. Working both as a freelancer and for agencies, he is also the editor for the independent publisher Milimbo, specializing in graphics and illustrated books, and a studio called Smoke, which creates graphics and editorials. Oller has released two books for children with Milimbo: *La luna sabe a pescao*, and *Y recuerda*. The elegant *Y recuerda (And Remember)* is a wordless book with three-color illustrations that create an amazing sense of depth with sparse information. Through impressive command of color and positive / negative space, Oller tells a visual story that parents will recognize as the classic Grimm Brother's *Red Riding Hood*.

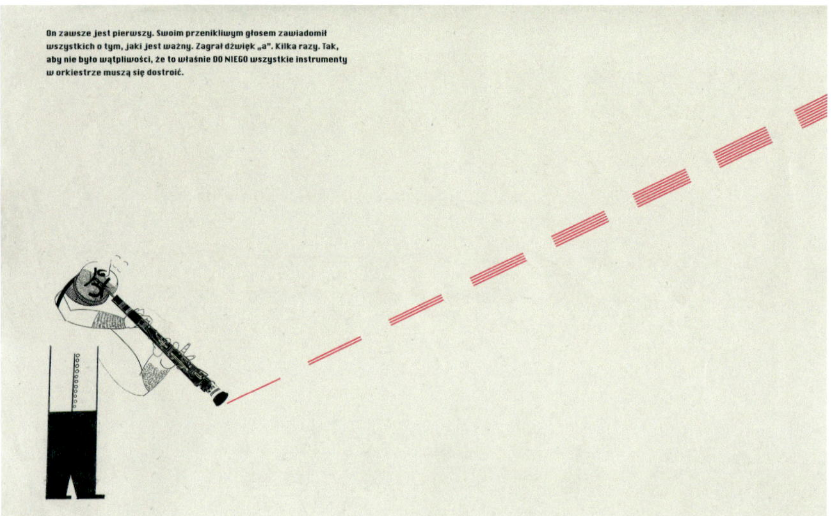

Wszystko gra
Author/Illustrator Anna Czerwińska–Rydel/Marta Ignerska
First Published 2011, Wytwórnia Publ./NIFC, Poland
Original Language Polish

marta ignerska

A graduate of Warsaw's Academy of Fine Arts, Polish illustrator Marta Ignerska has worked as a graphic designer, art director, and freelance illustrator before launching her own graphic design/illustration studio in 2011. She has made images and animations for magazines, newspapers, advertisements, exhibitions, cultural events, and books. She designs and illustrates books for many publishing houses worldwide, including Znak, LektorKlett, Éditions du Rouergue, Media Vaca, Orecchio Acerbo, and many more. Her newest books for children are *Wszystko gra* (Wytwórnia, 2011), *Bruxas: Beijos e outros encantos* (Editora Biruta, 2011), and *How to Twist Tongue: Handbook for Children* (Znak, 2010).

„To nie sztuka grać tak, żeby wszyscy wokół tańczyli" - parsknął obój. „Ważne, aby umieć ich potem prowadzić" - powiedział z wyższością. „Dlatego to JA jestem pierwszy!".
„Pożar! Pożar!" - ostrzegała wciąż trąbka.
„Spalamy się w miłości" - płakały altówki.
„W miłości szczęśliwej" - marzyły wiolonczele.
„Do szczęśliwej miłości, na uroczystym ślubie, grają skrzypce" - orzekł koncertmistrz, a zespół skrzypiec mu zgodnie przytaknął.
Nagle ktoś wszedł.

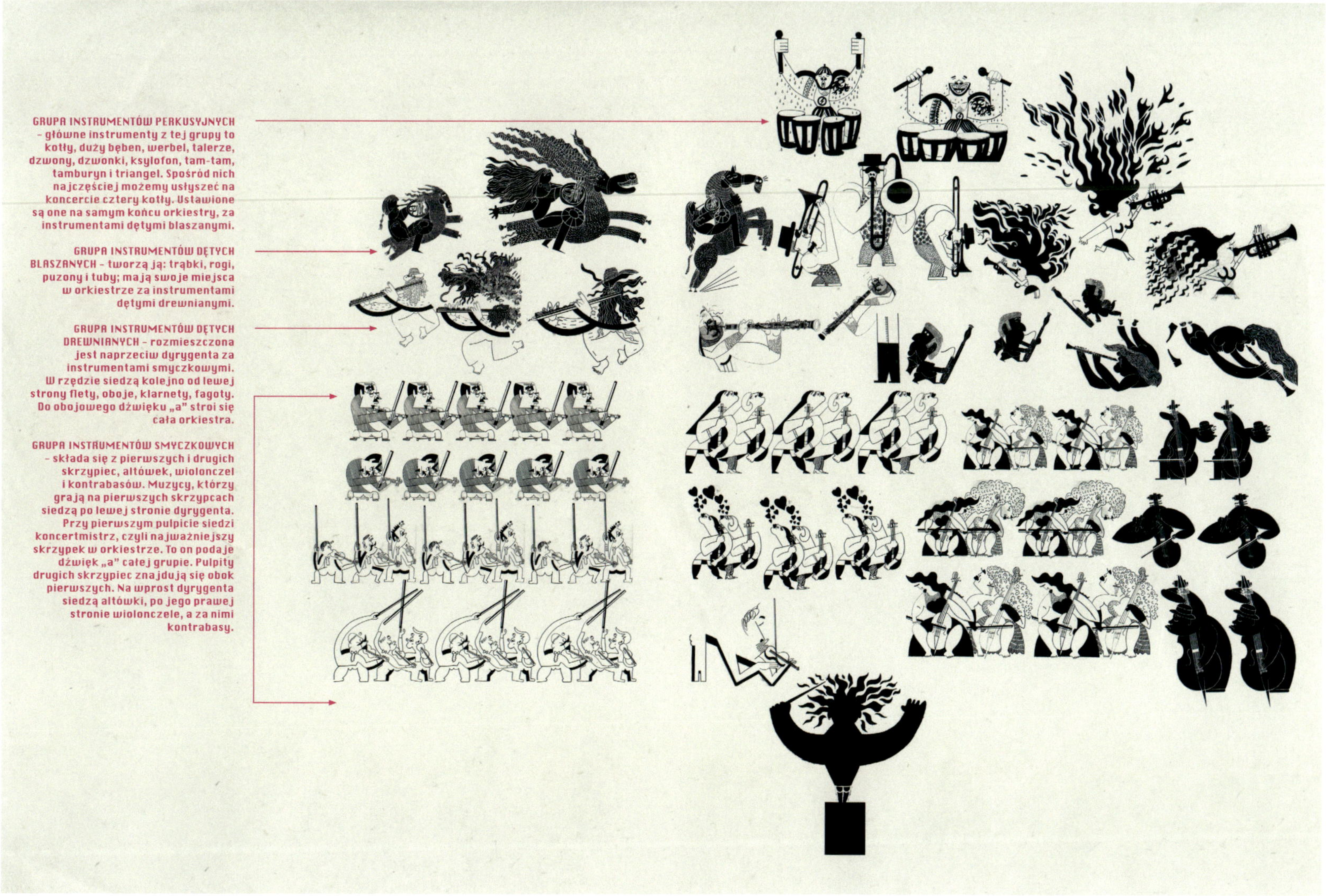
GRUPA INSTRUMENTÓW PERKUSYJNYCH - główne instrumenty z tej grupy to kotły, duży bęben, werbel, talerze, dzwony, dzwonki, ksylofon, tam-tam, tamburyn i triangel. Spośród nich najczęściej możemy usłyszeć na koncercie cztery kotły. Ustawione są one na samym końcu orkiestry, za instrumentami dętymi blaszanymi.
GRUPA INSTRUMENTÓW DĘTYCH BLASZANYCH - tworzą ją: trąbki, rogi, puzony i tuby; mają swoje miejsca w orkiestrze za instrumentami dętymi drewnianymi.
GRUPA INSTRUMENTÓW DĘTYCH DREWNIANYCH - rozmieszczona jest naprzeciw dyrygenta za instrumentami smyczkowymi. W rzędzie siedzą kolejno od lewej strony flety, oboje, klarnety, fagoty. Do obojowego dźwięku „a" stroi się cała orkiestra.
GRUPA INSTRUMENTÓW SMYCZKOWYCH - składa się z pierwszych i drugich skrzypiec, altówek, wiolonczel i kontrabasów. Muzycy, którzy grają na pierwszych skrzypcach siedzą po lewej stronie dyrygenta. Przy pierwszym pulpicie siedzi koncertmistrz, czyli najważniejszy skrzypek w orkiestrze. To on podaje dźwięk „a" całej grupie. Pulpity drugich skrzypiec znajdują się obok pierwszych. Na wprost dyrygenta siedzą altówki, po jego prawej stronie wiolonczele, a za nimi kontrabasy.

Diverse [1,2,3,6,7,8]
Illustrator Gémeo Luís
Personal Works 2006–2010

Erva-palavra [4]
Illustrator Gémeo Luís
First Published 2007, Gailivro, Portugal
Original Language Portuguese

1

2

3

4

5

6

7

8

O conta-gotas [5]
Illustrator Gémeo Luís
First Published 2010, Edições Eterogémeas, Portugal
Original Language Portuguese

gémeo luís

Portuguese illustrator Luis Mendonça works under the artist alias of Gémeo ("Twin") Luís, perhaps alluding to the double or shadowed nature of his work. Luis's beautiful, delicate, paper-cut illustrations often incorporate the shadow of the three-dimensional paperwork in the reproductions. Currently based in Porto, the artist exploits the powerful storytelling tool of the paper-cut silhouette in books such as *O quê que quem (Who Which What)* which won the Portuguese National Illustration Award in 2005. Luis is one of the founding members of Edições Eterogémeas and a professor at the Porto Faculty of Fine Arts.

Migrando
Author/Illustrator Mariana Chiesa
First Published 2010, Orecchio Acerbo, Italy
Original Language Italian
For Amnesty International.

mariana chiesa

Mariana Chiesa comes from La Plata, Argentina. Born in 1967, she eventually moved to Barcelona in 1997 and to Italy in 2008, where she currently lives near Bologna. She works as an illustrator for publishers based all over the world: Media Vaca, Zoolibri, Sins Eentido, and L'Association. Among many notable titles, her *No hay tiempo para jugar (There's No Time to Play)* was prized by the Monaco International Library in 2005 and published in Spain by Media Vaca and in Italy by Zoolibri. This book in particular, written with Sandra Arenal, demonstrates Chiesa's interest in social issues, which she depicts using varied artistic languages – engraving, painting, and drawing.

interview
larry lempert
jury member
astrid lindgren
memorial award

Honoring the memory of Sweden's best-loved and most translated author – children's book writer and vociferous advocate of children's rights Astrid Lindgren – the world's highest endowed award for children's and young adult literature sets out to promote interest in reading and storytelling around the world.
To this end, the Astrid Lindgren Memorial Award (ALMA) is open to living authors, illustrators, oral storytellers, and those who promote reading, albeit with a strong emphasis on an open, varied, and, most of all, truly international selection.
Aided by 400-plus nominating bodies around the world, each year the award's engaged and engaging jury take on the daunting, exhaustive, and impressive task of scouring the entire planet for the latest challenging, rewarding, and offbeat books, traditions, or projects that further artistic integrity and boost understanding between cultures and people.
In the spirit of Lindgren's deeply humanist stance – no whitewashing or skirting of complex and provocative topics – ALMA's selection has given us a decade of delightfully bold, unpredictable, and inspiring winners. Here, long-time ALMA jury member (and head of Sweden's International Library) Larry Lempert takes us through the award-giving process – including a quick peek into the future of children's books.

COULD YOU TELL US LITTLE BIT ABOUT YOURSELF AND WHAT BROUGHT YOU TO THE ASTRID LINDGREN MEMORIAL AWARD (ALMA) IN THE FIRST PLACE?

In 1975, I started working as a children's librarian in Tyresö, a small municipality outside of Stockholm. Back then, I began to focus on children's literature and programs to promote reading, and I have been involved in related issues ever since. During these 35-plus years, I have also served as a member of the IBBY (International Board on Books for Young People), the International Federation of Library Associations and Institutions' (IFLA) section for children's libraries, and joined national teams on publishing, literary subsidies, and working promotions. In 2003, I was made head of Sweden's International Library, an institution that offers books in more than 120 languages – books from all over the world that give us great insights into the current state of children's literature from around the globe. Naturally, my own experience – having children myself – also helps greatly in pursuit of this mission!

IS SERVING ON THE ALMA JURY A FULL-TIME JOB? HOW DO THESE JURY-RELATED DUTIES OCCUPY YOUR TIME – BOTH DURING AWARD SEASON AND IN BETWEEN CEREMONIES?

While my main job and responsibility remains with the International Library, being part of the jury does require a substantial chunk of my time. Although the jury only meets around once a month, we spend a lot of the time in between reading, evaluating work designed to promote literacy, learning about children's literature ... Each of our meetings lasts at least a day or two, giving us plenty of time to discuss, argue, learn, and broaden our knowledge of the award's candidates.

CONSIDERING THE SHEER WEALTH OF INTERNATIONAL CANDIDATES AND WORTHY PROJECTS ON OFFER, YOU COULD NOT POSSIBLY EVALUATE ALL POTENTIAL NOMINEES YOURSELVES, BUT RELY ON A BROAD RANGE OF NOMINATING BODIES FROM AROUND THE WORLD. HOW DO YOU PICK THESE INSTITUTIONS?

Straight after the jury was formed, we started to look for suitable nominating bodies from all corners of the world, aided by the ALMA administration. Our goal: to get the best possible and most comprehensive overview of the current state of children's literature, programs to promote reading, storytelling traditions, etc. Our current tally stands at around 400 nominating bodies across the globe, representing expertise, knowledge, deep insights, and – most of all – commitment in the field.

WHICH ASPECTS OF THE AWARD AND SELECTION PROCESS DO YOU, PERSONALLY, FIND MOST IMPORTANT AND REWARDING?

I love the way the award throws a spotlight on children's literature and promotes discussions that generate new knowledge – both for myself and for the rest of the world. It is really gratifying to see how many people around the world care about children's literature and spreading literacy!

La Visite de Petite Mort (page 123)
Author/Illustrator Kitty Crowther
First Published 2004, Pastel, Belgium
Original Language France

Le Petit Homme et Dieu (page 120)
Author/Illustrator Kitty Crowther
First Published 2010, Pastel, Belgium
Original Language France

WHEN IT COMES TO BUYING CHILDREN'S BOOKS—A REALM WHERE PARENTS WANT TO DO AND PICK WHAT IS BEST FOR THEIR KIDS—AWARDS AND OFFICIAL RECOMMENDATIONS CAN PLAY A MAJOR ROLE. DO YOU FEEL THAT SOME BOOKS ARE BEING PUBLISHED WITH AN EYE TO POTENTIAL AWARDS (IN TERMS OF STORYLINE OR VISUAL STYLE)?

While I can't speak for other award-giving bodies, creators or publishers would have a hard time pandering to the ALMA jury. After all, we have been very unpredictable in our choice of award winners, so I don't think that publishers could identify any particular topics or styles to pick or commission future winners. At the same time, this award also serves as an eye-opener: it demonstrates that it is worth going with daring storylines or unknown authors, not just the established ones or the "safe option."

I BELIEVE THAT CHILDREN'S BOOKS, LIKE ALL BOOKS, BUILD BRIDGES.

WHILE WE ARE ON THE SUBJECT OF DARING STORYLINES, HOW DO SUCCESSFUL AUTHORS ADDRESS ADULT OR UNCOMFORTABLE TOPICS LIKE LOSS, DEATH, OR MENTAL HEALTH? AND HOW DO CHILDREN REACT TO SUCH STORIES? SHOULD THESE SUBJECTS BE TACKLED AT ALL IN (PICTURE) BOOKS FOR A PRESCHOOL AUDIENCE?

Loss, death, joy, and love are topics that exist all around us and remain part of our lives. By taking these intense situations and emotions seriously and by writing about them with empathy, any author can address them in a way that is suitable for children. I think it is vital that we, as adults, discuss and share these topics with our kids and don't just leave them alone with their thoughts when the situation arises. In the end, age does not matter: by reading aloud or together and sharing our views and reactions, we can give the child a chance to work through their own emerging thoughts and feelings.

LOOKING BACK—WITH TEN YEARS OF EXPERIENCE AND ALMA AWARDS UNDER YOUR BELT—WHERE DO YOU SEE FURTHER SCOPE FOR IMPROVEMENT?

These first ten years have been truly amazing. They have introduced us to the sheer richness in children's literature and related fields around the world. Now we know how little we know—and how much more there is to explore. Our most vital mission is to show the nominating bodies just how important they are—after all, they are our eyes and ears in the world. And we should place even higher emphasis on supporting the rights of children to have access to stories and literature.

YOU MENTION THE IMPORTANCE OF ACCESS TO LITERATURE. WHAT ROLE (CULTURAL, EDUCATIONAL, OR OTHERWISE) DO CHILDREN'S BOOKS PLAY IN SOCIETY?

I believe that children's books, like all books, build bridges. Bridges that give us friends, knowledge, and access—ultimately, they will help to bring about a more peaceful world. By reading and learning more about children and/or conditions in a world we know little about, finding friends in books, and discovering places, children learn to feel empathy, love, and grief. We learn to grow through children's books!

Naturally, children are influenced by the world around them, i.e., by their parents, teachers, librarians, friends, commercials, etc. Our duty as adults is to open the world of stories to our children, stories told in many different ways, stories from many different countries. We are talking about children's rights to stories—not adults' wishes to influence!

One of the largest problems I see in the realm of children's literature is that it is so local or, should I say, regional. I would love to see literature from around the world achieve a broader reach. As Astrid Lindgren once said, "Good literature gives the child a place in the world—and the world a place in the child."

* * *

Le Petit Chaperon rouge
Author/Illustrator Joël Pommerat/Marjolaine Leray
First Published 2009, Actes Sud/Théâtre de Sartrouville et des Yvelines–CND, France
Original Language French

marjolaine leray

Marjolaine Leray originally comes from a small village in the Loire-Atlantique region of France, where she was born in 1984. Moving to Paris later on, she studied visual communications at the Duperré School. Her illustrations for Joël Pommerat's *Le petit chaperon rouge*, a reinterpretation of Little Red Riding Hood, were published by Actes Sud in 2005. A 40-page hardback illustrated and written by Leray followed in 2009: *Un petit chaperon rouge* retells the same classic story in a edgy and unexpected new way and received wide acclaim. The book has been translated by Sarah Ardizzone and republished in English by Phoenix Yard Books in London, United Kingdom.

Hänsel und Gretel
Author/Illustrator Grimm Brothers/Sybille Schenker
First Published 2011, Minedition, Germany
Original Language German

sybille schenker

Sybille Schenker's pursuit to become an illustrator brought her to New York in 2007. After completing a master's degree at the School of Visual Arts, Schenker has worked for the past several years as a freelance illustrator and designer for international clients, recently returning to her native Germany. Born in Nuremberg in 1980, Schenker's natural talent for drawing has been honed to a fine skill for creating books and illustrations. Now based in Berlin, the artist uses many techniques, including cut paper, transparencies, etchings, and line drawings in her many books for children, such as her recent retelling of the classic folktale *Hansel and Gretel*.

Hänsel und Gretel
Author/Illustrator Brothers Grimm/Lorenzo Mattotti
First Published 2011, Carlsen, Germany
Original Language German

lorenzo mattotti

Lorenzo Mattotti was born in Italy in 1954. After studying architecture, he decided to devote himself to comics, and is recognized today as one of the most outstanding international exponents of the art. His works have been published everywhere in print, including the covers of the *New Yorker*, *Le Monde*, and *Süddeutsche Zeitung*; he has worked in fashion, advertising, and film; and his books are translated all over the world. Mattotti's work has evolved with a continuing coherence, though always within the eclectic tradition of constant innovation. As for children he has illustrated *Pinocchio*, *The Pavilion on the Links*, and *Eugenio*, which won the Grand Prize of Bratislava in 1993.

The Blue Bird [1]
Author/Illustrator Cho Sunkyung
First Published 2009, Somebooks, South Korea
Original Language Korean

Lalala [2,3]
Author/Illustrator Cho Sunkyung
First Published 2011, Somebooks, South Korea
Original Language English

cho sunkyung

Cho Sunkyung is a picture book illustrator based in Seoul, who also makes animated movies and stand-alone drawings and paintings. His colorful and complex books for the Korean Borim Press include *Magohalmi*, completed in 1996, and the more recent *Underground Garden*, released in 2005. The incredibly detailed images in these books and others Sunkyung create depth through their unbelievable use of perspective and carefully rendered contrast between light and shadow. One of Sunkyung's few projects in black and white, he illustrated the classic story of *Hansel and Gretel* for a film by Korean director Lim Phil-sung (*Hansel and Gretel*, 2007).

Semidisegnitelodico
Illustrator Philip Giordano
Illustration 2012, Online Exhibition

philip giordano

Born in Celle, a small coastal town near Liguria, Italy, freelance illustrator Philip Giordano attended the Brera Academy of Fine Arts in Milan and the European Institute of Design. In 2004, Giordano was selected for the Bologna Children's Book Fair, and thanks to the visibility he gained there, he started working for children's book publishers. His first books were with Hodder in London and Zoolibri in Italy. In 2006 and 2009, he won the Figures Futur competition at the Montreuil Children's Book Fair, and in 2010 he won the International Illustration Award in Bologna. His books have been translated around the world, including France, South Korea, Thailand, China, Spain, and Japan, where he currently resides.

The Nice Crazy Forest [1,4]
Author/Illustrator Eric Giriat
Stickers 2010, Dona Fusion, Brazil
Original Language Portuguese

1

2

3

4

Atelier portraits [2,3]
Author/Illustrator Eric Giriat
First Published 2010, Réunion des Musées Nationaux/Sarbacane, France
Original Language French

Un éléphant peut en cacher un autre [5]
Author/Illustrator François David/Eric Giriat
First Published 2005, Sarbacane, France
Original Language French

eric giriat

It would be hard to find an illustrator more interdisciplinary than Eric Giriat. Beginning with serial illustrations for *ELLE* magazine in 1996, Giriat's work has expanded to various magazines, book covers, advertisements, fashion design, and children's books in Germany, the United States, Russia, and his native country of France. Eric's versatile capabilities are shown in these fields by way of collage, gouache, colored pencils, and line drawings, which he creates while living between Paris and Berlin. One of his most beloved kid's books is called *La Tête perdue de Monsieur Mue*, published by Éditions Sarbacane in 2009.

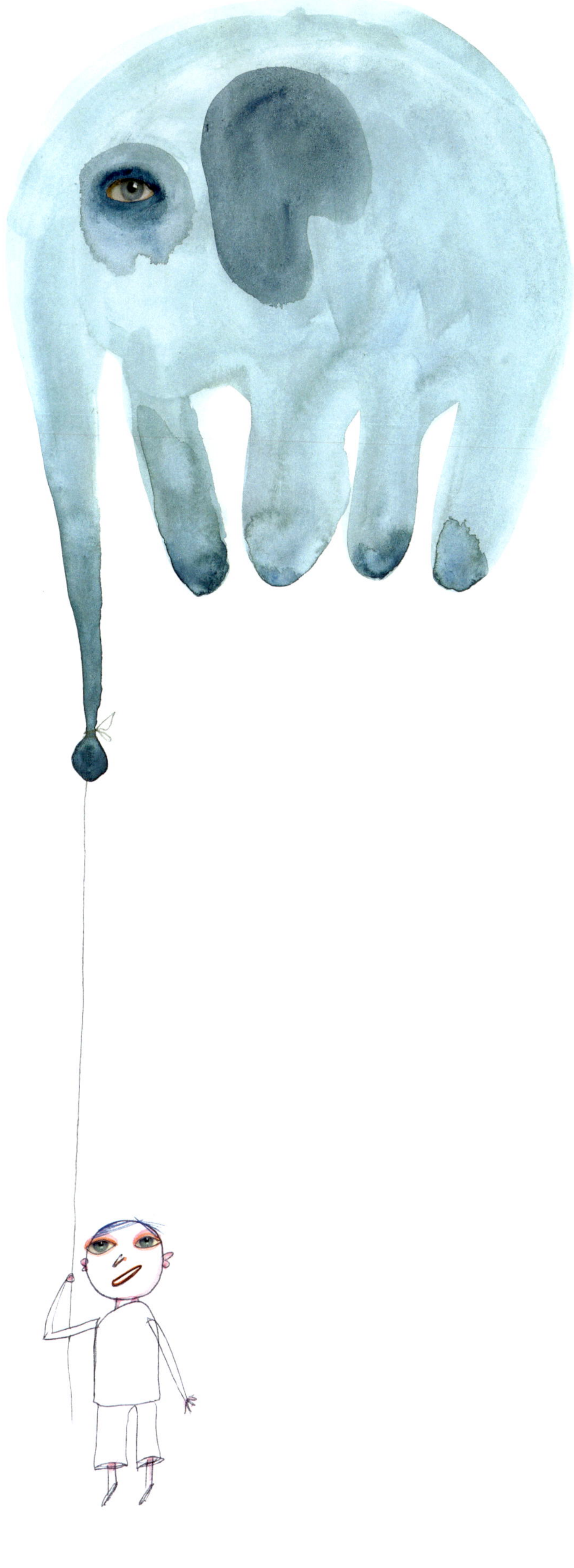

Untitled [1,2,3]
Illustrator Chiara Armellini
Illustrations 2012

Ti faccio a pezzetti [4,5]
Author/Illustrator Chiara Armellini
First Published 2012, Topipittori, Italy
Original Language Italian

chiara armellini

Chiara Armellini was born in the northeast of Italy in 1985. Currently based in Vincenza, she makes illustrations using a variety of techniques, such as monotypes, etchings, screen-prints, rubber stamps, acrylic paint, and sometimes programs like Photoshop and Illustrator. Her children's book, *Ti faccio a pezzetti (I Cut You Into Pieces)* was recently published by the Italian publishing house Topipittori. Fascinated with animals and their behavior, Armellini has created a book featuring all the fantastic features found in the animal kingdom: beaks, feathers, fur, claws, fangs, scales, fins, and wings. The unusual book offers a series of incisive riddles for children to solve.

Waterlife
Author/Illustrator Rambharos Jha
First Published 2011, Tara Books, India
Original Language English

rambharos jha

The dazzling picture book *Waterlife* features Mithila art, a vibrant and delicate form of folk painting from Bihar in eastern India. Its artist, Rambharos Jha, grew up on the banks of the legendary river Ganges, and, surrounded by lush fields and ponds, developed a fascination for water and waterlife. In this visually stunning book, Jha creates an unusual artist's journal, adapting the motifs of the Mithila style to express his own vision of life and nature. He frames his art with a playful text that evokes both childhood memory and folk legend. The specially crafted *Waterlife* is silkscreened by hand on handmade paper.

2

La Sœur du soleil [1]
Author/Illustrator Bahiyyih Nakhjavani/Sandrine Thommen
First Published 2010, Actes Sud, France
Original Language French

La Fleur du mandarin [2]
Author/Illustrator Bahiyyih Nakhjavani/Sandrine Thommen
First Published 2009, Actes Sud, France
Original Language French

Voyage [3]
Author/Illustrator Caroline Pellissier/Sandrine Thommen
Unpublished
Original Language French

sandrine thommen

Young illustrator Sandrine Thommen was born in 1986 and, after studying at the École Estienne in Paris, attended Strasbourg's esteemed School of Decorative Arts. There she met author Bahiyyih Nakhjavani, with whom she discovered a common artistic sensibility. Two books have resulted from the duo's fruitful collaboration: *La Fleur du mandarin* and *La Sœur du soleil*, both published by Actes Sud Junior. Thommen's drawings perfectly accompany Nakhjavani's extraordinary stories in incredible, mesmerizing detail. In addition, Thommen creates picture books on her own that tell wordless stories, such as *L'Arbre*, published in 2012 by the French company Autrement Jeunesse.

The Night Life of Trees
Author/Illustrator
Bhajju Shyam, Durga Bai, Ram Singh Urveti
First Published 2006, Tara Books, India
Original Language English

bhajju shyam durga bai ram singh urveti

The Night Life of Trees is a book created together by Bhajju Shyam, Durga Bai, and Ram Singh Urveti. Their intricately drawn visions of trees fill the pages of this sumptuous book of art and folklore from the Gond tribe in central India. In Gond belief, trees stand in the middle of life and contain many spirits. Recreated from original art by Urveti, Shyam, and Bai, three of the finest living artists of the Gond tradition, the book is a tribute to the majesty of trees and to old ways of relating to the natural world. Each painting is accompanied by its own poetic tale or myth – narrated by the artists themselves to recreate the familiarity and awe with which the Gond people view the cosmos.

Akiko la courageuse [4,5]
Author/Illustrator Antoine Guilloppé
First Published 2010, Picquier Jeunesse, France
Original Language French

antoine guilloppé

Antoine Guilloppé was born in Chambéry, France, and currently lives in the Montrouge region near Paris. After studying drawing at the Emile Cohl School in Lyon, he became an illustrator for youths, and since then has illustrated numerous covers for editions of novels published by Thierry Magnier, Readers International, Rageot, and more. He has published several kids' books as an author-illustrator, including four popular books for Philippe Picquier about a character named Akiko: *Akiko la curieuse*, *Akiko la rêveuse*, *Akiko l'amoureuse*, and *Akiko la courageuse*. Guilloppé has also collaborated on books with various authors such as Beatrice Fontanel and Ghislaine Roman.

Plein soleil

Author/Illustrator Antoine Guilloppé
First Published 2011, Gautier-Languereau, France
Original Language French

Como agua [1,3]
Author/Illustrator Eduardo Abel Gimene/Cecilia Afonso Esteves
First Published 2009, Ediciones Del Eclipse, Argentina
Original Language Spanish

Poemas de alta mar [2]
Author/Illustrator Canela/Cecilia Afonso Esteves
First Published 2011, Editorial Comunicarte, Argentina
Original Language Spanish

cecilia afonso esteves

El libro de los fantasmas [4]
Author/Illustrator Nelvy Bustamante/Cecilia Afonso Esteves
First Published 2011, Editorial Ruedamares, Argentina
Original Language Spanish

Poetic and contemplative, the collage-based graphic work of Cecilia Afonso Esteves has appeared in numerous books for children. Among many other distinctions, the Argentinian artist was a finalist in the Children's Book and Illustration categories of the Spanish Book Design Awards in 2011. Most recently, she illustrated the book *A cozinha da dona nininha (Dona Nininha's Kitchen – Companhia das Letrinhas, 2012)*, which beautifully accompanies a text by Brazilian author Lená Loureiro. In addition to publications, Esteves also creates animations, prints, and jewelry, and her fine art has appeared in various international exhibitions.

Mrs Muffly's Monster [1]
Author/Illustrator Sarah Dyer
First Published 2008, Frances Lincoln, United Kingdom
Original Language English

The Girl with the Bird's-Nest Hair [2]
Author/Illustrator Sarah Dyer
First Published 2009, Bloomsbury, United Kingdom
Original Language English

sarah dyer

Sarah Dyer graduated from London's Kingston University with a bachelor's in illustration in 2001. Her first book, *Five Little Fiends*, won the Bronze Smarties Prize and the United Kingdom Reading Award. The book was an international success, translated into eight different languages. Since then, Dyer has written and illustrated six more books, including *Clementine and Mungo*, among others, for Bloomsbury and *A Monster Day at Work*, among others, for Frances Lincoln. These books, with their quirky and stylized humor, are simple stories that pose complex questions. When Sarah is not writing and illustrating, she teaches at Kingston and Middlesex Universities.

FEATURING...
(in no particular order).

Chaffinch

Barn Owl

Greenfinch

Song Thrush

Dove

Chiffchaff

Mallard (drake)

House Martin

Domesticated Duck

Swallow

Pigeon

J'attends

… de grandir

1

Moi, j'attends [1,2,4]
Author/Illustrator Davide Cali/Serge Bloch
First Published 2005, Sarbacane, France
Original Language French

Poèmes et Chansons de Jacques Prévert [3]
Author/Illustrator Jacques Prévert/Serge Bloch
First Published 2008, Bayard Jeunesse, France
Original Language French

3

2

… qu'elle me dise oui.

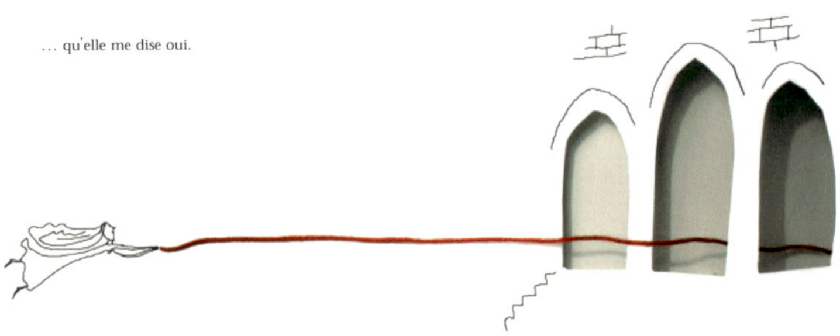

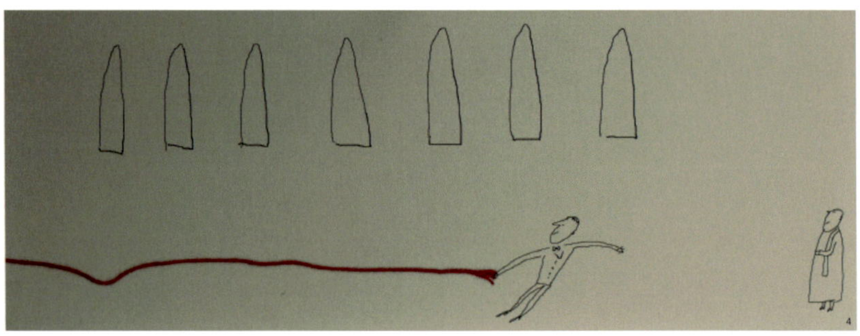

4

L'Ennemi [5]
Author/Illustrator Davide Cali/Serge Bloch
First Published 2007, Sarbacane, France
Original Language French

serge bloch

Drawing primarily in ink for over 30 years, Serge Bloch is one of the outstanding illustrators of his generation. Enrolling at university in Strasbourg in 1978 at age 22, Bloch found his calling, and since then has worked across all media, publishing in newspapers and magazines, creating work for advertisers and private clients. His art has appeared in exhibitions around the world, and his work has been translated into several languages. Bloch creates beloved characters that appear in books, comics, and animated series, including the wildly popular Max and Lili, Samsam, and Toto, all of whom every child in France is likely familiar with. In 2005 he received the Gold medal of the Society of Illustrators.

The
Davide Cali | Serge Bloch
Enemy
3206
3214
WILKINS farago
amnesty international australia

5

1

2

3

4

Un bestiario de la prehistoria [1,3,4]
Author/Illustrator Ianna Andréadis
First Published 2008, Petra Ediciones, Mexico
Original Language Spanish
First limited edition of 100 copies by Les Trois Ouses, 1998, France

SSSS: Snake Art and Allegory/Manasa, légendes de serpents indiens [2]
Author/Illustrator Gita Wolf/Ianna Andréadis
First Published 2010, Tara Books, India/Musée du Quai Branly, France
Original Language English/French translation by Elisabeth Foch

ianna andréadis

Ianna Andréadis (* Athens, 1960) is a Greek artist and photographer who has created many books and extremely diverse international projects with worldwide participation. In 2004, she coordinated a digital photo project called "The World Around a Flame / Olympic Truce 2004", which was exhibited in Athens during the Olympic Games that year. She studied both fine arts and archaeological art history, embarking on various journeys and projects that combine her wide-ranging interests, such as her travels through East Africa with publisher Franck Bordas which resulted in a series of drawings and paintings. Based in France, she has published a group of art books for children in African wax textile.

Ente, Tod und Tulpe
Author/Illustrator Wolf Erlbruch
First Published 2007, Verlag Antje Kunstmann, Germany
Original Language German

wolf erlbruch

Wolf Erlbruch, born in 1948, studied graphic design and worked as an illustrator in the advertising industry before he started in the late 1980s to write and illustrate children's books. His numerous awards include the 2003 Gutenberg Prize from the city of Leipzig and both the German Children's Literature Award in 1993 and its Special Award in 2003. Most recently, he received the esteemed Hans Christian Andersen Award in 2006. Just a few of his notable beloved books include *Die große Frage*, *Leonard*, *Das Bärenwunder*, and *Die Werkstatt der Schmetterlinge*. The German illustrator is also a professor at the University of Wuppertal.

Holding puppies
Karin Eklund, 2012, www.keeart.co.uk
MA Children's Book Illustration/
Cambridge School of Art at Anglia Ruskin University

interview martin salisbury on the history, make-up and psychology of picture books

Avid illustrator – and instigator of the United Kingdom's first master's program in children's book illustration – Martin Salisbury likes to bridge the gap between visual arts and academic theory in his explorations of children's literature. As part of his course, and with the insightful compendium and dissection of the genre, "Children's Picturebooks: The Art of Visual Storytelling" (co-authored by Morag Styles – Laurence King Publishing, 2012), Salisbury looks beyond the pretty pictures to uncover the history, make-up, and peculiar psychology of visual storytelling as a cultural agent. Peppered with plenty of case studies and techniques, his publication explores how picture books shape us, how artists shape them, and how the market, in turn, shapes the artists. And while his publication does provide plenty of hands-on advice on how to craft a creative and coherent narrative, it also delves deep underneath the surface – from early cave paintings to modern-day irreverence – in order to present an artistic and anthropological approach to visual storytelling.

LET'S START WITH SOME BACKGROUND INFORMATION: WHAT PROMPTED YOU AND YOUR CO-AUTHOR, MORAG STYLES, TO TACKLE THIS PARTICULAR SUBJECT?

Morag Styles and I are from very different backgrounds. While we both have a passion for picture books, we approach them from very different perspectives. Morag is a Professor of Children's Poetry at the University of Cambridge, Faculty of Education, and has written widely on children's picture books – from the perspective of an academic and in relation to the world of education and children's literature. She is especially interested in how children respond to picture books. With her and Professor Maria Nikolajeva, the Children's Literature Research Centre here in Cambridge boasts two of the best-known academics in the field.

I, on the other hand, come from an art school background and studied Illustration at the Maidstone College of Art under Gerald Rose, an award-winning picture book author and illustrator who is still going strong. For many years, I worked as a freelance illustrator, mainly in children's publishing, and also taught part time alongside my professional work. But when I designed and launched the MA Children's Book Illustration program at the Cambridge School of Art (at Anglia Ruskin University), it started to take over my life, so I went full time!

Morag, Maria, and I have been collaborating across these two institutions for some time, arranging joint research seminars for our respective students and co-supervising PhD students. We had been talking about doing a publication on picture books for years – and finally got around to it. Our main aim was to bring these two worlds, practice and theory, a little bit closer together. Illustration has always been poorly served in terms of critical theory, and it is only very recently that picture books have been taken a little more seriously as part of our artistic culture. When it comes to children's picture books, we still tend to see either "how-to" books or heavily academic theories, so we decided to fill this gap!

TO GIVE US SOME CONTEXT ON YOUR OWN PREFERENCES, COULD YOU NAME THREE SEMINAL PICTURE BOOKS THAT – IN YOUR OPINION – HAD THE GREATEST IMPACT ON THE EVOLUTION OF THE GENRE?

Many key picture books have influenced the development of illustrated children's books over the years, decades, and centuries. Many of Randolph Caldecott's books were essential in advancing the possibilities of "counterpoint" between words and pictures and giving the image a greater autonomy. Maurice Sendak, of course, remains the undisputed genius of the picture book form, and it is difficult to overestimate the importance of *Where the Wild Things Are*. I would say that John Burningham, Bruno Munari, and Leo Lionni are also key figures, as is Ezra Jack Keats for introducing a more socially and racially inclusive world to illustrated children's books.

HISTORICALLY SPEAKING, WHEN DID CHILDREN'S BOOKS START TO APPEAR? HOW HAVE VISUAL STYLES AND TOPICS CHANGED OVER TIME? WHICH BOOKS OR THEMES ARE STILL CONSIDERED PERENNIAL CLASSICS, WHILE OTHERS HAVE FALLEN BY THE WAYSIDE?

I don't think it is possible to pinpoint a single moment when children's books came into their own as a distinct literary genre. It has certainly happened at a different pace in different cultures and is only just happening in some. Each culture has its own particular take on childhood, and so children's

Untitled
Trudi Esberg, 2012, trudiesberger@me.com
MA Children's Book Illustration / Cambridge School of Art at Anglia Ruskin University

literature will have evolved accordingly. Of course, as with other media, books for children have become less patronizing, less didactic. At the same time, ideas of what is suitable for children, visually and conceptually, vary enormously across cultures and time. We have progressed from cruel cautionary tales through Victorian sentimentality and excessive morality to cosy 1950s family stereotyping and postmodern self-referentiality.

The concept of perennial classics and longevity interests me greatly. While I do greatly bemoan the predominately conservative nature of children's publishing in the U.K., it is noticeable that a greater proportion of picture books seem to stand the test of time than in many other cultures. Visiting the Bologna Children's Book Fair every year, as well as the Far East, I find myself greatly seduced by the picture books published in e.g., France, Belgium, Italy, Spain, Scandinavia, Japan, and South Korea. However, it seems that many of these only ever make it through one small print run – and then they are never seen again. So, this is a bit of a mystery. If I knew what makes a timeless classic, I would be a successful publisher or picture book creator! But the best, most lasting books seem to be the ones where the picture book maker (writer? illustrator? author? – we still don't have a word for it!) leaves space between word and image for the imagination to roam. Judith Kerr's *The Tiger Who Came to Tea*, John Burningham's *Granpa* and *Come Away from the Water, Shirley* are great examples.

WRITER? ILLUSTRATOR? AUTHOR? – WE STILL DON'T HAVE A WORD FOR IT!

ASIDE FROM THE "TIMELESS" CRITERION, COULD YOU TAKE US THROUGH THE KEY STAGES OF CREATING A SUCCESSFUL PICTURE BOOK FOR CHILDREN?

I'm afraid I can't! The successful element depends entirely on the individual creator's vision. I am very suspicious of anything that suggests a formula. However, I would say that it is important to think of creating a picture book in a similar way to composing a piece of music or a poem. Usually, everything starts with a few storyboard sketches. This involves laying out the book's (often 32) pages as a series of spreads, composed and drawn very roughly in the guise of tiny thumbnail designs. The next stage tends to involve making a small maquette or dummy of the book by stapling the pages together. This will give a greater sense of the book's flow and pace in relation to the page-turning experience. These processes allow for constant revision and changes to the overall flow and perception. Often, it takes a great many storyboards and dummies before things start to feel just right.

ON A MORE GENERAL NOTE, WHAT ARE THE RULES OF PICTURE-BOOK MAKING – AND WHEN IS IT OKAY OR EVEN IMPERATIVE TO BREAK THEM? WHAT WOULD BE OBVIOUS BEGINNER'S MISTAKES OR MORE SUBTLE STUMBLING BLOCKS?

There are many common mistakes made by those setting out to create a picture book for the first time. The first is the belief that it is easy. More than most areas, picture-book creation suffers from the "I could do that" perception. There are many obvious mistakes, e.g., trying to write a narrative or sequence in words and then illustrating it in a way that means the words and pictures are saying the same thing. Usually, the process of "writing" or making a picture book has to be one that involves thinking about words AND pictures right from the start. A very common mistake is to make perfect pictorial double-page compositions and then ask yourself, "Right, now where shall I put the words?" Right from the start, the words need to be an integral part and shape of the layout – a visual element that is as important as anything else that appears on the page. The spread's composition should seem "wrong" before the text is added.

LET'S SAY YOU ARE AN ASPIRING, TALENTED, AND – AS YET – UNKNOWN ILLUSTRATOR WITH A STRONG NARRATIVE STREAK. HOW WOULD YOU GO ABOUT GETTING YOUR IMPENDING MASTERPIECE PUBLISHED? ANY PRAGMATIC ADVICE ON THE BUSINESS SIDE?

When trying to get published, getting your work seen by an editor or designer is the first major hurdle. This is difficult. Publishers are generally bombarded with plenty of mediocre work and can be difficult to get hold of. I found that it helps greatly to have a personal contact or reference of sorts. If you come from a well-regarded art school or course, that also helps. It is important to research any publishing house thoroughly before you make your approach. You have to know what they publish and why your particular work would sit well with them. On a more practical side, a simple dummy / maquette of the picture book is the best way to present it, with some of the spreads finished but most remaining as roughs. Remember, a dummy is the only way to experience the full page-turning experience. I have found that some publishers are happy to see an idea presented on an iPad, but most of them seem to hate it. Perhaps this is just a generational thing! Attending the Bologna Children's Book Fair, which takes place in March every year, is a great way to get a sense of the business side of things and to show your work to interesting publishers (albeit in a rather competitive and potentially demoralizing context!).

GENERALLY SPEAKING, WHAT MAKES IMAGES SO EFFECTIVE AS A STORYTELLING DEVICE?

I think images and words in partnership are especially effective, although "silent" picture books are increasingly common. More and more often, authors

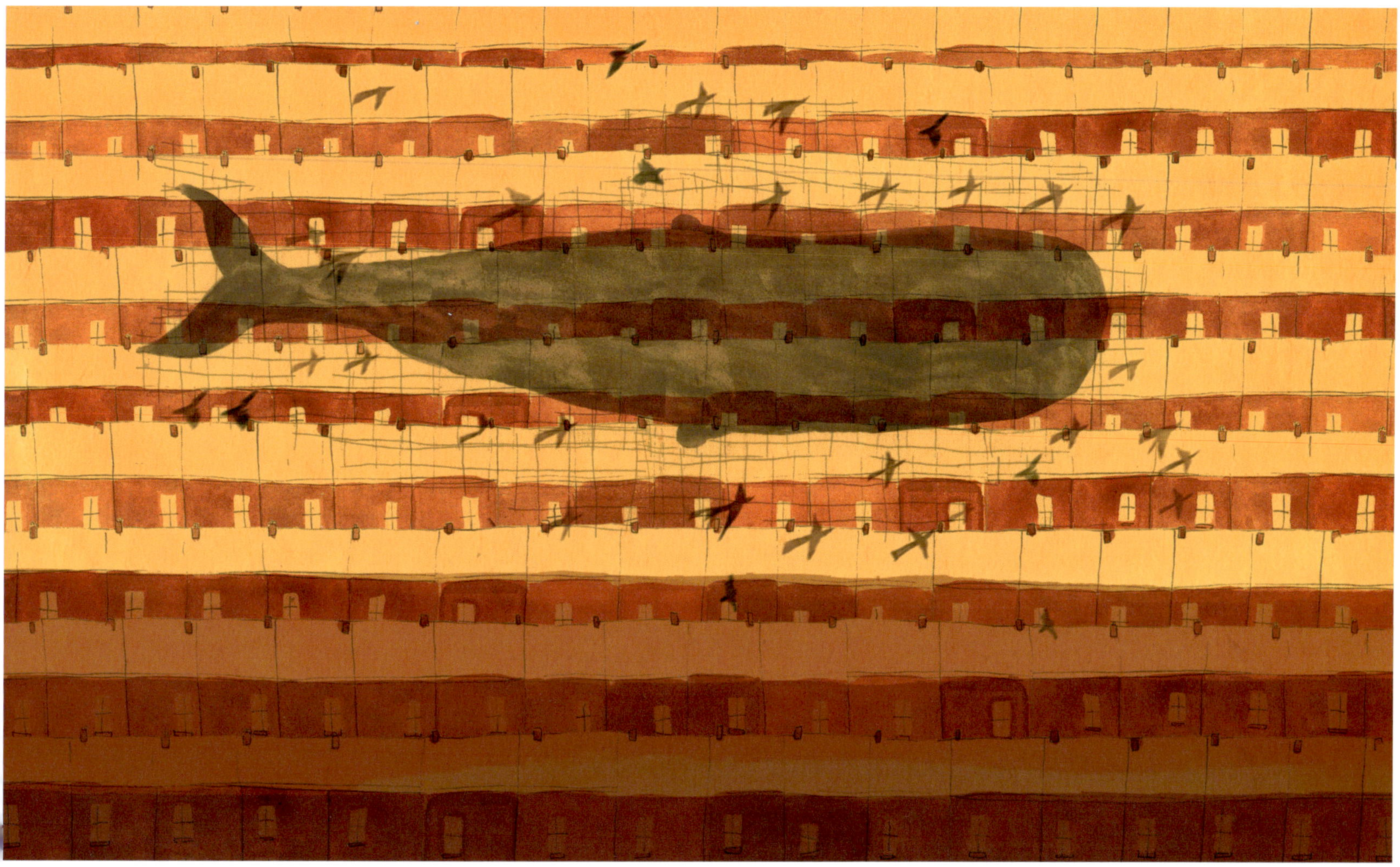

Fish in net
Jenni Desmond, 2012, www.jennidesmond.com
from *Red Cat, Blue Cat*, 2012, Blue Apple Books, United States
MA Children's Book Illustration/
Cambridge School of Art at Anglia Ruskin University

are playing around with the word-image dynamic, allowing pictures to subvert or contradict the words and vice versa. The narrative image maker can lead the eye around the page and manipulate time and space in many ways.

THAT SOUNDS INTRIGUING. DO CHILDREN'S BOOKS HAVE THEIR OWN LOGIC, SYNTAX, OR GRAMMAR?

In many ways, picture books certainly have their own grammar. Traditionally, they come in 32 pages (although publishers are less and less rigid about this nowadays), and this means that you need to condense a visual sequence into around 12 spreads – once the end papers, title page, and copyright pages have been taken into account. The process of "reading" pictorial narrative from left to right (in the West at least) means that the rhythm, pace, and ebb and flow of the picture book need to be plotted carefully around this format and the act of page-turning within it – a form of stage direction if you will. In a way, the picture book becomes a theater where the maker is the director, stage manager, actor ... and in total artistic control!

HOW DO CHILDREN DEVELOP VISUAL LITERACY WHEN THEIR BRAINS ARE STILL FORMING AND THE WORLD AROUND THEM IS AN UNFAMILIAR PLACE FULL OF WONDERS? HOW DO THEY PERCEIVE COLORS, PATTERNS, AND DEPICTIONS?

One of the problems of trying to research young children's responses to imagery is the fact that they don't have the language to express what they are experiencing. And of course they are, just like us, individuals – with equally individual tastes and responses. But it seems clear that they develop the ability to process pictorial sequences very early on. In fact, this seems to be an ability that we – quite often – have to relearn as adults! My guess is that, even if everything in the images is unfamiliar, children are making their own sense of things. On a basic but important level, a picture book will allow time for the eye to travel around the page and explore shape, color and form. The key thing is that the speed is not dictated externally, as with many screen-based media.

WITH THIS IN MIND, HOW DO PICTURE BOOKS IN TURN INFLUENCE AND SHAPE THE MENTAL DEVELOPMENT OF PRESCHOOL READERS?

There are many ways that picture books influence the minds of young readers. Much is made of the educational and moral messages that are conveyed by stories in general, but I am more interested in the way that a library of picture books educates children in the world of art. After all, this is often a child's first introduction to the visual arts: the picture book serves as a personal, private art gallery, held in the hand, to be revisited over and over again. While we cannot know for sure, a close encounter with quality picture books at an early age must surely have an impact on aesthetic taste and sensibility. This is another area that is very difficult to research. But as adults, we all seem to have very strong attachments to the picture books that we grew up with. It is one of the reasons for the huge interest in collecting older children's books.

LOOKING BACK – AT THE BROTHERS GRIMM, ET AL. – CHILDREN'S BOOKS OFTEN USED TO CONTAIN A, BY TODAY'S STANDARDS, SHOCKING NUMBER OF TALES THAT WERE LESS THAN POLITICALLY CORRECT AND FILLED WITH VIOLENCE, GRATUITOUS CRUELTY, MISOGYNY, ETC. DID OR DOES THIS AFFECT A CHILD'S ETHICS OR MORALS?

Children seem to have a limitless capacity to absorb and handle all manner of things that we might worry about. In recent generations, we have become much more protective and censorious. While we would not wish to return to the days when children's books promoted the chopping off of thumbs if they were being sucked, I think a lot depends on the tone with which such cruelty is portrayed. Roald Dahl's enormous popularity reflects his complete absence of patronizing language and a joy in "incorrectness" that children adore. I think we could afford, certainly in the West, to be a little less protective.
Children are individuals and will be frightened and delighted in their own individual ways. But it is clear that all children do love to be frightened! I would say the books that delight the most are those that allow the child to feel "in on the secret." In other words, children love books that allow them to see things in the pictures that are not acknowledged in (or are sometimes contradicted by) the words. As the adult reads the words, the child discovers a whole other world in the pictures.

AS THE ADULT READS THE WORDS, THE CHILD DISCOVERS A WHOLE OTHER WORLD IN THE PICTURES.

IN THIS SPIRIT, ARE THERE ANY PARTICULAR SUBJECTS OR STORYLINES THAT WORK SURPRISINGLY WELL OR NOT AT ALL? WHY DO CERTAIN – AND CERTAINLY UNUSUAL – SUBJECTS FIND A CAPTIVE AUDIENCE DESPITE ALL ODDS?

Of course, the theory is that there are only seven stories in the world and that every story is no more than a variation on one of these. But not all picture books are narrative, and nonfiction is being addressed in increasingly entertaining and inventive ways. There are inevitable trends that come and go in popularity in the mass-market sector, with much imitative work being commissioned. But of course the big successes always come from the most unexpected sources. Characters are very important. Every publisher is looking for a new character that captures the public imagination. Uncomfortable or

Osos blancos; Quieto / Quiebre
Soledad Veliz, 2012, hermanaojo.carbonmade.com
MA Children's Book Illustration /
Cambridge School of Art at Anglia Ruskin Universityt

"difficult" topics have been addressed in picture books in many ways. In my view, the most successful ones are the ones that deal with the topic in the subtlest of ways. Jo Empson's *Rabbityness* (Child's Play, 2012) is a wonderful example of a picture book that deals with death in a sensitive way – and celebrates life.

ARE THERE OBVIOUS DIFFERENCES IN THE USE OR PERCEPTION ACROSS DIFFERENT CULTURES OR GEOGRAPHIES? DO AUDIENCES REACT DIFFERENTLY OR DEMAND DIFFERENT APPROACHES? WHAT PROMPTS STRONG NATIONAL OR INTERNATIONAL PHENOMENA AND TRENDS?

In my view, the picture book is a key element of the cultural fabric of any society. Each culture will have its own heritage of children's book art. But the extent to which this is appreciated and supported by arts organizations varies greatly around the world. The U.K., for example, has an extremely rich heritage, but it saddens me to see that much of the original artwork is kept in Japanese museums rather than here. Artists like Brian Wildsmith and John Burningham are revered in Japan and in constant demand to visit. Quentin Blake is doing his best to address this with his efforts to set up the House of Illustration in London, which will contain archives of illustrators' work, including his own, and present regular exhibitions.

THE PICTURE BOOK IS A KEY ELEMENT OF THE CULTURAL FABRIC OF ANY SOCIETY

We can learn a lot from the many smaller cultures that place great importance on their picture books as art. The Flemish Literature Fund has organized wonderful traveling exhibitions and catalogs of work. The Norwegian government finances initiatives to ensure that indigenous artists and writers are represented in this field. This kind of support has led to some ground-breaking picture books that have emerged without the dead hand of committee-led editing – and the results have won international awards and influenced the development of the genre as a whole.

At the same time, I think that, initially, the fall of communism led to an over-eager embracing of what might be termed Disneyfication in some of the Eastern bloc countries. This reaction was then followed by a realization that their own, often rich, traditions were being lost. We have seen some wonderful studies and exhibitions of Soviet picture books recently; their didactic, propaganda-led nature has its own peculiar and particular charm.

Anecdotally speaking, I continue to observe many cultural differences, but of course I am stereotyping when I mention the Scandinavian / northern European freedom from fear of tackling dark subjects, French and Italian philosophical lyricism, or American postmodernism. Right now, China does not seem to have a tradition of picture books as entertainment and I expect to see this huge market take off spectacularly in the future.

FINALLY, HOW WILL THE MARKET FOR PICTURE BOOKS CHANGE?

Of course, one of the main preoccupations right now is the role of downloadable apps and e-books in the picture-book market. At the moment, no one seems to know quite what their impact will be, but everyone is running around saying, "We should be doing something." One thing, however, is clear: printed picture books are becoming increasingly beautiful in their production with ever greater attention to the physical, tactile "holding" quality of the books as artifacts, in gloriously varied sizes and shapes. This process is carving out the territory of the book as a beautiful thing; a thing distinct from the screen that provides us with information but doesn't allow us to own, feel, or interact with it in the same way. Until very recently, most picture book apps were rather banal in their conception, concentrating on trying to shoehorn commercially proven books into an alien format with minor digital bells and whistles. It reminds me of the period immediately after the arrival of Photoshop when everything looked the same as designers decided they were now illustrators. Once the people who were most resistant to it (i.e., the ones who weren't seduced by technology) began to learn to use the program, however, things started to get interesting.

Similarly, app development is still rather dominated by those who are interested in the technology at the moment. But that, too, is changing as artists begin to move in and explore the possibilities. There is no reason for an app to be limited in terms of "page" numbers or linearity. We need to stop using the word "book" in this context and perhaps speak of something like "story apps." Nevertheless, it seems likely that the printed picture will endure and continue to evolve as a much loved and increasingly culturally appreciated art form.

* * *

Rikki-tikki-tavi (in Kipling illustrado)
Author/Illustrator Rudyard Kipling/Isidro Ferrer
First Published 2011, Kalandraka, Spain
Original Language Spanish

isidro ferrer

Isidro Ferrer studied drama and scenography. He combines his work as a graphic designer with intensive work in other visual fields such as illustration for adults and children, comics, TV cartoons, and publishing. Based in Spain, he has published more than 30 books, and his work has been the subject of individual exhibitions in cities around the world. Most notable of the many awards he has received are: the Lazarillo Illustration Prize, third prize at the Chaumont International Poster and Graphic Design Festival, a Promax Gold award, three AEPD awards, a LAUS award, and the Spanish National Design Award. Since 2000 he has been a member of the Alliance Graphique Internationale.

NEWS
ANCE

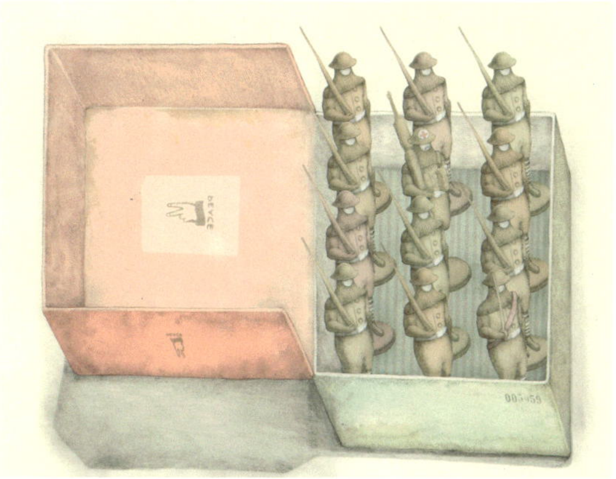

El soldado de plomo
Author/Illustrator Hans Christian Andersen/Page Tsou
First Published 2012, Fundación SM, Spain
Original Language Spanish

page tsou

Originally from Taiwan, Page Tsou is currently based in London. With a master's in communication art and design from the Royal College of Art, he has exhibited his work in cities worldwide and has received significant international recognition – most recently, Best of Show at *3x3*'s 2011 Professional Show, the 2011 *Communication Arts* 52 Award, and the coveted first prize at the 2011 Bologna Children's Book Fair. He was honored in Bologna for his book *Dancing Feathers*, inspired, like much of Tsou's work, by such diverse influences as traditional Chinese ink painting, Japanese comics, street art, and 1960s steampunk.

Flight [1]
Author/Illustrator Narges Mohammadi
Unpublished 2011

Deer Hunter [2]
Author/Illustrator Narges Mohammadi
Unpublished 2011

I Am Not Afraid [3]
Author/Illustrator Soroor Kotobi/Narges Mohammadi
First Published 2009, Behnash, Iran
Original Language Persian

The Hero's Trick [4,5]
Author/Illustrator Mohammad Reza Yousefi/Narges Mohammadi
First Published 2007, Behnash Iran
Original Language Persian

narges mohammadi

Narges Mohammadi was named one of the Edgiest Artists of the 2008 Bologna Children's Book Fair, where she exhibited her illustrations for the kids' book *I Am Not Afraid*. The story is about a chick inside an egg who is afraid to hatch because of the sounds outside. Eventually the chick hatches and finds the world to be very beautiful. Mohammadi's illustrations create a beautiful world indeed – told primarily through printing and collage, her stories aim to present something entirely unique each time. Living and working in her native Tehran, Mohammadi is receiving growing recognition abroad, receiving, for example, the CJ Picture Book Award in 2010.

1

3

4

5

The Princess

Author/Illustrator Fereshteh Najafi

First Published 2008, Shabaviz Publishing Company, Iran

Original Language Persian

When I Was a Kid [1]
Author/Illustrator Fereshteh Najafi
Unublished 2011

Swiming in the Lake and Nosy Man [2]
Author/Illustrator Fereshteh Najafi
Calendar 2012, Italy

Tara [3]
Author/Illustrator Fereshteh Najafi
Unpublished 2011

fereshteh najafi

Fereshteh Najafi was born in Tehran, Iran, in 1974. She has a bachelor's in graphic design and a master's in illustration from Tehran Art University. Najafi has created about 30 illustrated books published in her country, Italy, and France, including the recent titles *La piccola pitrice* (Coccole e Caccole, 2010), *Le Roi Bahram* (Grandir, 2010), and *Un giorno* (Arco, 2011). She has also participated in numerous exhibitions around the world, such as the Biennial of Illustration in Bratislava, Slovakia, and the International Exhibition of Illustrations for Children in Sarmede, Italy. Additionally, Najafi has won several prizes, including second prize at the Numa Illustration Festival in Japan in 2009.

1000 zanimaux [1]
Author/Illustrator Morteza Zahedi
First Published 2011, Réunion Des Musées Nationaux, France
Original Language French

morteza zahedi

The compositionally creative and eclectic imagery dreamed up by Morteza Zahedi has brought attention to his work both in his native Iran and abroad. Born in 1978 in the seaside city of Rash, Zahedi graduated in painting from Azad's University of Art and Architecture. He has won both the Tehran Illustrators Biennale and the Belgrade Illustrators Biennale. Zahedi writes, "There are two types of artists: the diligent and the spontaneous ... I belong to the second type." This spontaneity is evident in the exuberant multi media illustrations that he has been creating for the last 10 years – focused on the elements of improvisation and play above rigid formal structure or singular style.

The Trip of a Butterfly [1,2]
Author/Illustrator Morteza Zahedi
First Published 2006, Shabaviz Publishing Company, Iran
Original Language Persian

With the Sun in My Eyes [4]
Author/Illustrator Morteza Zahedi
First Published 2012, Groundwood, Canada
Original Language English

4

2

1

Zapatos para Estubigia y otros cuentos [2,4]
Author/Illustrator Alfonso Alcalde/Tomas Ives
First Published 2011, Pehuén Editores, Chile
Original Language Spanish

Perros héroes [1,3]
Author/Illustrator Mario Bellatin/Tomas Ives
First Published 2011, Pehuén Editores, Chile
Original Language Spanish

tomas ives

Chilean artist and illustrator Tomas Ives has a stark, stunning, and memorable graphic style. Also a marketing and art director, Ives's clients include *Rolling Stone Chile, Le Monde Diplomatique Chile,* and Canal 13. In 2011, Santiago-based Pehuén Editores printed *Perros héroes,* a children's book by famed novelist Mario Bellatin with illustrations by Ives. *Dog Heroes* tells the story of an immobile man and his 30 dogs, who are grotuesque and slightly frightening creatures. The book is a mysterious, unusual tale full of black humor, in which the style of Bellatin is matched perfectly by Ives's illustrations.

3

Rapido [1]
Author/Illustrator Jean-Luc Fromental / Joëlle Jolivet
First Published 2011, Helium, France
Original Language French

Oups! [2]
Author/Illustrator Jean-Luc Fromental / Joëlle Jolivet
First Published 2009, Helium, France
Original Language French

Zoologique [3]
Author/Illustrator Joëlle Jolivet
First Published 2002, Seuil Jeunesse, France
Original Language French

joëlle jolivet

Joëlle Jolivet was born in 1965 in the Val-de-Marne region of France. After studying graphic art and advertizing at the School of Applied Arts in Paris, she became interested in engraving and painting, and spent a year doing a lithography course at L'École des Beaux Arts. This led her to lino-cutting, which has remained her main mode of expression to this day. In addition to her own books, she has illustrated numerous book covers and works occasionally for the press. Jolivet may be best known for her children's book *Zoo-ology* (Roaring Book Press, 2003), which has been translated into various languages. She lives and works in Ivry-sur-Seine, close to Paris.

Moby Dick [4]

Author/Illustrator Herman Melville and Philippe Jaworsky / Joëlle Jolivet
Paper Engineering Gerard Lo Monaco
First Published 2010, Gallimard Jeunesse, France
Original Language French

Een griezelmeisje
Author/Illustrator Edward van de Vendel/ Isabelle Vandenabeele
First Published 2006, Uitgeverij De Eenhoorn, Belgium
Original Language Dutch

isabelle vandenabeele

Highly acclaimed Belgian illustrator Isabelle Vandenabeele was born in 1972. Her career began in 1998 when she illustrated the book *Reuze* for author Gregie de Maeyer. Since receiving an honorable mention for this first project, she has accumulated numerous awards for her work. She accumulated many skills while studying for seven years at the St. Lucas Institute in Ghent, and prefers to work with lithography, woodcuts, and etchings – opting always for simplicity over detail. Writer and publisher Marita Vermeulen describes Vandenabeele's imagery as "essential images limited to basic lines ... creating nuances and atmospheres, turning shapes and figures into exciting compositions."

1

2

3

Anansi and Death [3]
Author/Illustrator Traditional/Kevin Vanwonterghem
Illustration of the African tale of Anansi and death.
This image was selected for the Figures Futur contest 2008, and was published in the catalog.

The Boy With the Green Eyes [1,2]
Author/Illustrator Pieter van Oudheusden/ Kevin Vanwonterghem
Unpublished
Based on the story of Peter Pan and Wendy.

Liefde kan niet zonder liefde [4]
Author/Illustrator Pieter van Oudheusden/Kevin Vanwonterghem
First Published 2010, De Eenhoorn, Belgium
Original Language Dutch

kevin vanwonterghem

Kevin Vanwonterghem was born in Ghent, Belgium, where he now lives and works. Vanwonterghem graduated in fine arts at St. Luc University in 2008, and currently works as an illustrator, muralist, and teacher. He has won various prizes for his artwork, including the Figures Futur 2008 Award and the Picturale 2007 Young Illustrators Award. He recently illustrated a book for young people with text by Pieter van Oudheusden called *Liefde kan niet zonder liefde (Love Cannot Live Without Love)* which was published by the Belgian company De Eenhoorn. His work for commercial clients has also appeared in magazines and newspapers such as *Rekto:Verso, Plots,* and the *NRC Handelsblad.*

4

The Tales of Number 3 and 7
Author/Illustrator Helen Jung Been Lee
Unpublished
Original Language Korean

helen j.b. lee

Born in Seoul in 1983, Helen Jung Bee Lee majored in communication design, but experimented with many other fields at Emily Carr University of Art and Design in Vancouver. After graduating she moved to Seoul and found a way to tell stories through pictures, creating her first book, *The Tales of Number 3 and 7*. The book explores the fact that in both the East and the West, certain numbers such as 3 and 7 have been considered to hold mysterious powers. When reading the book from right to left, readers learn about the number 3 in Eastern culture; reading from left to right, the use of the number 7 in Greek and Roman civilizations and Christianity is presented.

1

Les Heureux Parents [1]
Author/Illustrator Laëtitia Bourget/Emmanuelle Houdart
First Published 2009, Éditions Thierry Magnier, France
Original Language French

Saltimbanques [2]
Author/Illustrator Marie Desplechin/Emmanuelle Houdart
First Published 2011, Éditions Thierry Magnier, France
Original Language French

emmanuelle houdart

Emmanuelle Houdart, born in 1967 in Switzerland, is a painter and illustrator of children's books. She began making books in 1996 after graduating from the École des Beaux-Arts de Sion and the School of Visual Arts in Geneva. Apart from occasional collaborations with various magazines and newspapers *(Libération, Le Monde, Sciences et Vie Junior)*, she has illustrated 20 books for youth at various publishers, and published five books that she both wrote and illustrated. Living and working in Paris, her books often feature animate objects and marvelously monstrous hybrid human-animal creatures, creating symbolic narratives through her frank, expressive lines.

Fantine
FERNANDE
Félicité
Cent ans de solitude G. G. Marquez
LE PIRE AVEC LE MEILLEUR R. DREYFUSS
L'un dans l'autre
OÙ SONT LES FEMMES ? P. JUVET
LA RELATION AMOUREUSE TOME I

Saltimbanques
Author/Illustrator Marie Desplechin/Emmanuelle Houdart
First Published 2011, Editions Thierry Magnier, France
Original Language French

interview johanna brock-lacassin on publishing rights and licensing

Let's say you have made a delightful picture book – and even managed to find a publisher. But what about the legal fine print? Who owns the rights to your little masterpiece? What do you do if someone else wants to use one of your images or ideas for a poster or play? And how do you spread the word – and images – across continents or language barriers? On hand to blaze a trail throught the legal jungle and the bewildering world of international publishing and rights management is Johanna Brock-Lacassin, the lovely and eminently patient foreign rights manager of French publishing houses Actes Sud, Rouergue and Thierry Magnier. In her everyday work, Johanna makes sure that enchanting books like Little Red Hood *(Marjolaine Leray),* New York in Pyjamas *(Frédérique Bertrand and Michaël Leblond) or* The Big Bad Wolf and Me *(Delphine Perret) reach a wider international audience – and shows that this vital discipline is not the dry subject you might expect!*

COULD YOU TAKE US THROUGH THE PROCESS OF INTERNATIONAL IMAGE AND RIGHTS LICENSING? WHAT EXACTLY DOES YOUR JOB ENTAIL?

I spend my entire day corresponding with foreign publishers! They send me specific rights requests or ask for books and PDFs to figure out if they would like to publish these works in their own language. In other words, I sell translation rights to foreign publishers who plan to release exactly the same book in another language and territory. This is all about precise negotiation and usually limits the publishing period (between five and ten years) and stipulates a particular language, area, and obviously – fee. Most of the time, licensees pay an advance against the royalties they will earn from selling this new language version. Once this advance has been covered, we receive a standard percentage of all subsequent earnings (between six and ten percent for children's books) from this edition. The agreement also determines if the foreign publisher will have the right to exploit any subsidiary rights such as, for example, book club rights, audio book rights, first and second serial rights, or electronic books rights.

While I deal with plenty of foreign publishers we have known for ages, I also try to discover new publishers – and contacts in the movie business for film rights – for possible future collaborations. After all, there is the lucrative niche of audio-visual rights when a film or television producer adapts one of our children's novels for the big screen, when one of our picture books is turned into an animated film or TV series – or when a theater company wants to turn a story into a play!

Another aspect of my work involves authorizing third parties to reproduce text or illustrations from our books – for example, this Gestalten publication. A lot of the time, we are contacted by French libraries who want to stage an exhibition and illustrate it with our images, or by French school book publishers who would like to publish extracts from our books in their own publications. A request like yours – i.e., a foreign publisher asking for select reproduction rights for certain images – tends to be more unusual.

To spread the word, I also create promotional materials for our books, i.e., book summaries or English-language catalogs, attend the genre's biggest international book fairs like the Frankfurt Book Fair (Germany) or the Bologna Book Fair (Italy), and follow up on networking opportunities with book and PDF mail-outs. Last but not least, there is the agreeable part of communicating with the authors to tell them where their books will be published and what kind of payment they can expect!

WHAT ARE THE TRICKY BITS AND PITFALLS?

Generally speaking, there is one important thing to keep in mind: Most of the time, it is the publisher, not the author, who needs to sign off on licensing deals as in France it is the publishing house that holds the respective rights of use. Naturally, we always ask our authors for permission before authorizing reproduction rights. However, I am only free to sell these rights because we have detailed written agreements with our authors. In France, the author's so-called "moral rights" are very strong and it is up to the publisher to defend these rights once the author has contracted them out to the publisher.

On a day-to-day basis, negotiating contracts with major American publishers can be the biggest challenge! Translation rights vary wildly on either side of the Atlantic, and American publishers usually expect to receive publishing

Les Heureux Parents
Author/Illustrator Laëtitia Bourget/Emmanuelle Houdart
First Published 2009, Editions Thierry Magnier, France
Original Language French

rights for the entire copyright period – something we cannot offer or allow. In addition, our contracts need to be governed by French or at least European law to safeguard our own contracts with our authors, while U.S. publishers would prefer contracts under American jurisdiction. So some great deals might fall through due to these cultural and legal differences.

Otherwise, we need to keep an eye on language territories. Let's say we sell the worldwide English rights to a U.K. publisher – and then find out that they won't publish the book on the U.S. market (or a Spanish publisher who does not serve the Latin American market). This is something we need to clarify in advance to make sure our books are available wherever people might want to enjoy them.

FROM YOUR OWN PERSONAL PERSPECTIVE, HOW HAS THE WORLD OF PUBLISHING CHANGED OVER THE LAST DECADE OR SO?

This is a tricky topic. I would say that publishing, in general, has become far more difficult than it was a mere 10 years ago. People tend to have less disposable income and spread their earnings across a wider variety of distractions (e.g., high-tech products), so they invest less in printed books. I find it harder to sell rights today than a decade or so ago. It is a little bit frustrating: on the one hand, new countries and territories are showing interest in our books, but on the other, the economies of nations like Spain or Greece don't allow local publishers to take the risk of buying the rights to foreign books.

YOU MENTIONED HIGH-TECH PRODUCTS. HOW DOES THE OVERALL SHIFT TOWARD DIGITAL PROCESSES AFFECT THE ENTIRE INDUSTRY – AND YOUR WORK IN PARTICULAR?

In France, it has not changed the book market a great deal, but the agreements between authors and publishers already cover electronic book editions. In my own line of work, I get the occasional request from foreign publishers to include an e-book option in their own language, so we have developed a corresponding contract clause. At the moment, we only approve such requests if the e-book version mirrors the printed product exactly – so no multimedia or enhanced editions.

HAVE YOU NOTICED ANY OBVIOUS TRENDS IN THE TYPE OF CHILDREN'S BOOKS OR ILLUSTRATION STYLES THAT WORK ESPECIALLY WELL (OR NOT) ON A NATIONAL OR INTERNATIONAL LEVEL? ARE THERE ANY COUNTRY-SPECIFIC DIFFERENCES?

Right now, mangas sell extremely well, as do novelty books and commercial young-adult novels. Then again, all countries have their own quirks and specialties. Both France and Belgium enjoy an ingrained "picture" culture and tradition with plenty of space and scope for sophisticated illustrations and picture books. In France, even adults buy beautiful picture books. Germany, on the other hand, has a strong market for illustrated books as gifts for adults and a tradition of more realistic illustrations, as do the Scandinavian countries, who also tend to prefer books with more text and more subversive storylines. Take Astrid Lindgren: back in the 1940s, her protagonists already disobeyed adults, while the first French translation of Pippi Longstocking had to change some of the passages to avoid shocking sensitive French parents!

THANK YOU FOR YOUR INSIGHTS! SO, IF I WAS AN ASPIRING AUTHOR OR ILLUSTRATOR, WHAT SHOULD I DO BEFORE I START?

Read a lot. Scour bookshops to get a feel for your target market. Try to discuss your idea with children's books publishers and meet art directors to present your work. Collaborate with other illustrators or authors!

FINALLY, WHY DO YOU ENJOY YOUR WORK?

AND I LEARN A LOT BY READING ALL OF THESE BOOKS!

I sell rights for books targeted at kids from zero to 20 years of age: picture books, novelty books, novels for first readers, young-adult novels, nonfiction for all ages, etc. And I learn a lot by reading all of these books! After all, they encompass both text and illustration and offer many layers and meanings hidden between these two levels of expression.

It is also fantastic to be able to travel and meet publishers from all over the world to discuss our favorite subject: books. Children's books can be so different depending on their country of origin and it is truly fascinating to find out why – and what might change in the future.

* * *

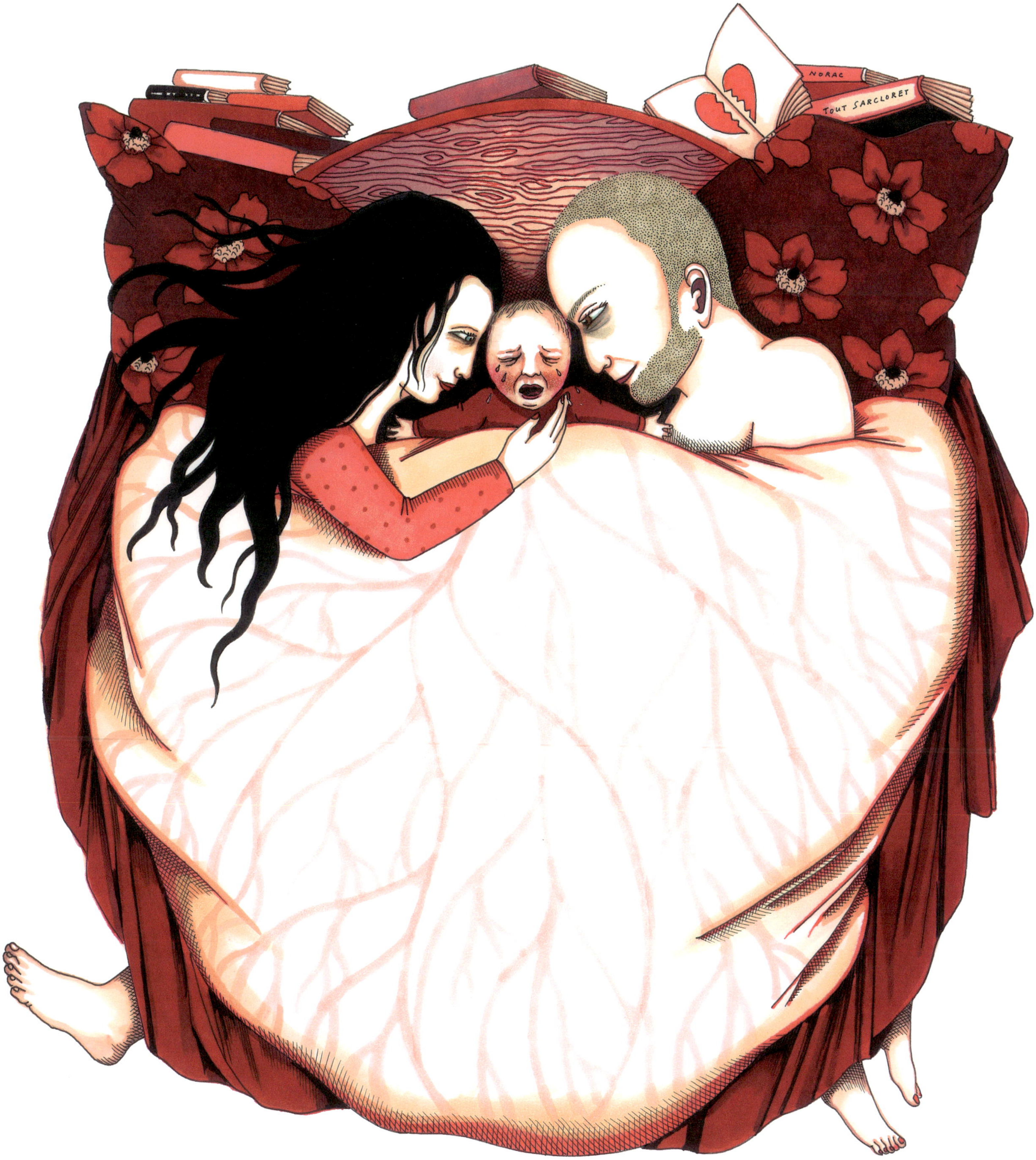
NORAC
TOUT SARCLORET

A min non me comas! [1,2,3]
Author/Illustrator Margarita del Mazo/Vitali Konstantinov
First Published 2011, OQO Editora, Spain
Original Language Galician

Giacomo di cristallo [4,5]
Author/Illustrator Gianni Rodari/Vitali Konstantinov
First Published 2011, Emme Edizioni, Italy
Original Language Italian

vitali konstantinov

Born in Odessa, Ukraine, Vitali Konstantinov studied architecture, graphic design, painting, and art history in both the former U.S.S.R. and Germany. He currently works as a freelance illustrator for children and adults, collaborating with various international clients and publishing houses. His reimaginings of classic texts by the likes of Daniil Kharms and the Brothers Grimm, as well as collaborations with contemporary best-selling authors, have been published around the world in Germany, Switzerland, Italy, Spain, Taiwan, South Korea, and the United States. He teaches at several European institutions, and in 2011 he was nominated for the German Youth Literature Prize.

3

2

Die Mondblume [1,3,4]
Author/Illustrator Einar Turkowski
First Published 2009, Atlantis/Orell Füssli, Switzerland
Original Language German

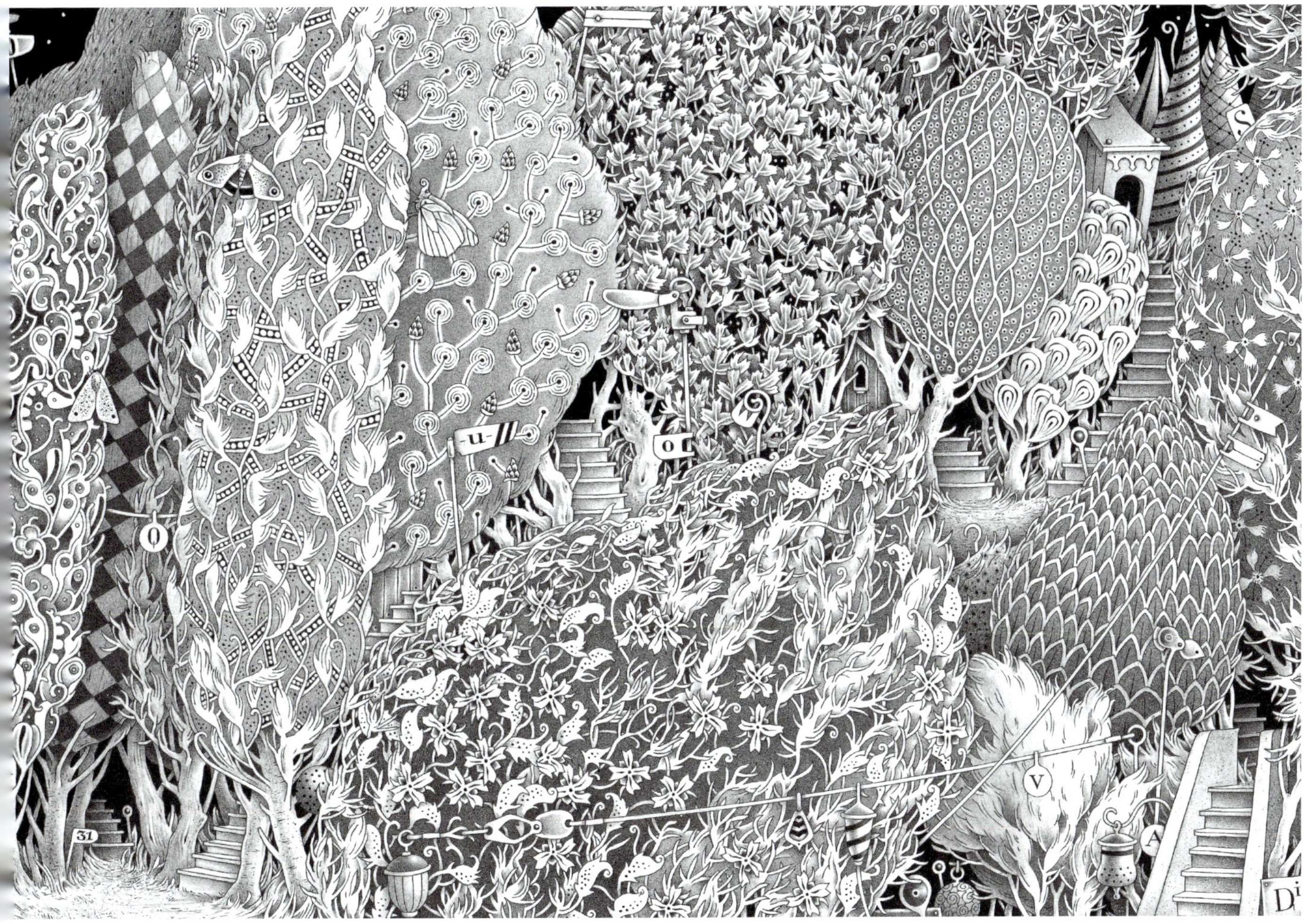

Es war finster und merkwürdig still [2]
Author/Illustrator Einar Turkowski
First Published 2007, Atlantis/Orell Füssli, Switzerland
Original Language German

einar turkowski

Born in 1972, Einar Turkowski studied in Hamburg before settling back near his native Kiel, where he works as a writer and illustrator. His work has been published internationally and received numerous awards—his first book alone (*Es war finster und merkwürdig still*, Atlantis, 2009) won the grand prize at the 21st Biennial of Illustration in Bratislava as well as *Crescer* magazine's 30 Best Children's Books Award. Turkowski's newest book, *Der rauhe Berg* (Atlantis, 2012), is exemplary of his whimsical, mysterious style. Turkowski draws his mesmerizingly complex pictures using only graphite, with attention to the minutest of details.

1

3

2

Los sueños del agua [1,4]
Author/Illustrator María del Carmen Colombo/Cristian Turdera
First Published 2010, Pequeño Editor, Argentina
Original Language Spanish

La Reina Mab, el hada de las pesadillas [2,3]
Author/Illustrator William Shakespeare/Cristian Turdera
Text adapted by Ruth Kaufman
First Published 2007, Pequeño Editor, Argentina
Original Language Spanish

cristian turdera

The multi-talented Cristian Turdera makes his home in Buenos Aires, where he was born in 1973. Turdera frequently combines illustration and graphic design in his work, and he enjoys illustrating everything: books, toys, notebooks, stickers, puzzles, posters, magazines, advertisements – to mention only a few. With children's books published in Argentina, France, Mexico, and Spain, Turdera still insists that he does not "draw for children." Rather, he makes books that, in their warmth and simplicity, are understandable to everyone. One of Turdera's most beloved books, *La Reina Mab* (Pequeño Editor, 2007), is a retelling of Shakespeare's timeless *Queen Mab*, with text written by Ruth Kaufman.

Troppo tardi [1]
Author/Illustrator Giovanna Zoboli/Camilla Engman
First Published 2010, Topipittori, Italy
Original Language Italian

Untitled [3,4,5]
Illustrator Camilla Engman
Illustrations 2012

C'era una volta la storia [2]
Author/Illustrator Giovanna Zoboli/Camilla Engman
First Published 2012, Topipittori, Italy
Original Language Italian

camilla engman

Swedish artist Camilla Engman was born in 1966 in the small town of Trollhättan and now lives and works in the city of Gothenburg. After studying at the Dome Art School and later at Gothenburg University's School of Design and Craft, Engman developed a signature style of illustration that has appeared in print, in exhibitions, and on various products. Commercially, she has worked for clients such as the *New York Times*, Converse, and Google. Emotional, evocative, and poignant, Engman's first children's book was released by Italian publisher Topipittori in 2010. *Troppo tardi (Too Late)* is the story of a child named Richard who feels like it is "too late" to go to sleep.

Mare en de dingen [1,2] Author/Illustrator Tine Mortier/Kaatje Vermeire
First Published 2010, De Eenhoorn, Belgium
Original Language Dutch

kaatje vermeire

Kaatje Vermeire (* 1981) discovered her talent for graphics and printmaking while studying graphic and advertising design at the Ghent Academy. The Flemish artist's first major illustration contract was for the book *De vrouw en het jongetje (The Woman and the Boy)*. Since then, the young artist has gone on to illustrate numerous other books, which have been translated into over 10 languages. Through a combination of collage, paint, drawing, and graphic techniques, Vermeire's unusual and striking images have earned her many awards, including the Grand Prix at the 2010 Illustration Bienniale in Ronse, Belgium.

Mannetje en Vrouwtje krijgen een kind [3,4]
Author/Illustrator Brigitte Minne/Kaatje Vermeire
First Published 2009, De Eenhoorn, Belgium
Original Language Dutch

Vorrei avere ... [1,2,3,4]
Author/Illustrator Giovanna Zoboli/Simona Mulazzani
First Published 2011, Topipittori, Italy
Original Language Italian

La fata Però nel bosco dei pini Perché [5]
Author/Illustrator Federica Campi/Simona Mulazzani
First Published 2011, Il Gioco di Leggere, Italy
Original Language Italian

simona mulazzani

Simona Mulazzani was born in Milan in 1964. She collaborates with leading Italian publishers including Rizzoli, Salani, Mondadori, Feltrinelli, Elemond, Einaudi, Editori Riuniti, Carthusia, Orecchio Acerbo, and Abitare Segesta. Her work is also published by various American, Japanese, and French companies: PHP and Publishing Shogaku-Kan, Bayard Presse, CO Sterling Publishing., Inc., and Harmony Books. Working with Gianluigi Toccafondo, Mulazzani has made commercials, television themes, and award-winning short films, such as La Pista, Le Criminel, and Woman Finding Love. Her illustrations have been exhibited in solo and group exhibitions. She currently lives and works in Pesaro, Italy.

Beaucoup d'enfants, en grandissant,
découvrent qu'elle n'est plus dans le tiroir
des jouets, plus dans la boîte à bonbons.
« Tant mieux comme ça », se disent-ils.

Elle était là, nichée
sous notre nez.
Une fois de plus,
on ne l'aura pas vue.

La Gigantesque Petite Chose
Author/Illustrator Beatrice Alemagna
First Published 2011, Autrement Jeunesse, France
Original Language French

beatrice alemagna

A native of Bologna, Italy, Beatrice Alemagna decided at eight years old to become a painter and writer. This early decision served her well: a winner of numerous prizes and creator of a long list of books and exhibitions, her work is by now appreciated the world over. Alemagna's books for publishers such as Seuil Jeunesse, Thierry Magnier, and Phaidon have been translated into 13 different languages. Her last two books for Phaidon, *The Bugs Next Door* (2012) and *Bugs in the Garden* (2012), are part of a series about bugs and are beautifully crafted from textured fabric samples.

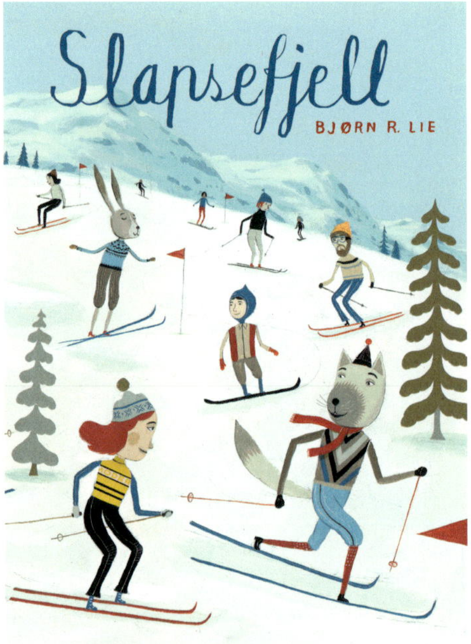

Slapsefjell
Author/Illustrator Bjørn Rune Lie
First Published 2008, Magikon, Norway
Original Language Norwegian

bjørn r. lie

Bjørn Rune Lie's charming drawing style is perfectly suited for illustrating kid's books. The Norwegian illustrator, born on the coastal town of Bergen, studied at the Falmouth College of Arts and now resides in Bristol, England. However, Norwegian nature is still very present in his work – the bursting good humor and skillful details remind us of the most joyful aspects of Scandinavian life. For instance, one book, *Slapsefjell* (Magikon, 2008), takes readers on a journey around the made-up Slush mountain ski village situated in the Norwegian Mountains. Both the book's menagerie of eccentric characters and their natural setting were hand-painted by Lie with loving detail.

Herrn Pastor
sien Koh

2

4

3

Herrn Pastor sien Koh [1]
Author/Illustrator Amrei Fiedler
First Published 2012, Carl Schünemann Verlag, Germany
Original Language German Dialect

Untitled [2,3,4]
Illustrator Amrei Fiedler
Personal Work 2012

amrei fiedler

Amrei Fiedler began drawing at a very early age in Hamburg, where she was born in 1984. After living in Buenos Aires, she decided to become a professional illustrator, and moved back to Hamburg to study illustration and begin her career. During her studies she dealt mainly with comics, multi media illustrations, cartoons, and children's books. In 2011, Fiedler completed her thesis work and is now a practicing illustrator. She has already completed two beautiful books for kids: the self-published *Fundhund*, and *Herrn Pastor sien Koh*, which came out with the Bremen-based Schünemann Verlag in 2012.

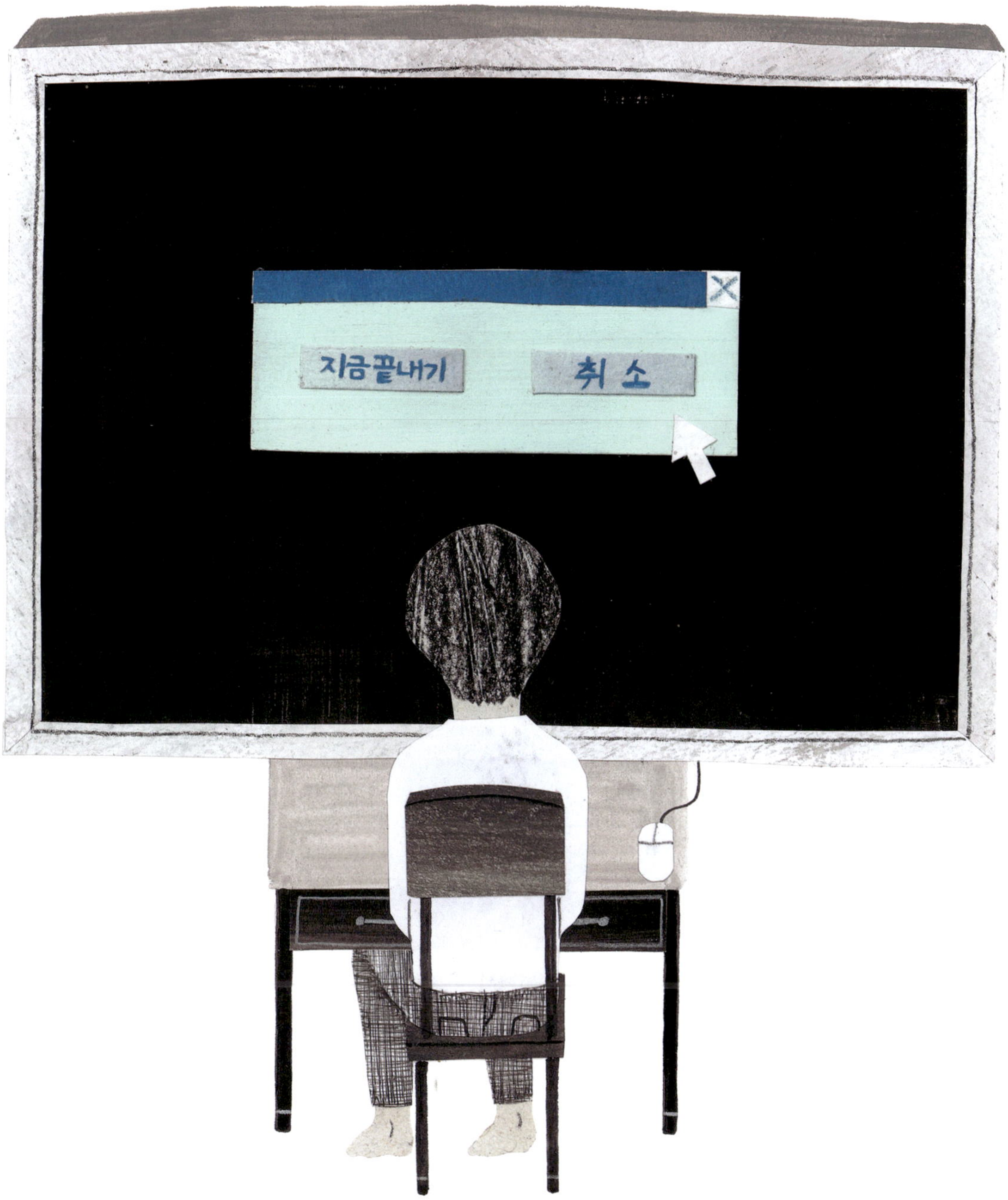

Star
Author/Illustrator Dajung Kim
First Published 2012, Maumsanchaek, South Korea
Original Language Korean

dajung kim

Dajung Kim is a freelance illustrator who lives in Seoul, South Korea. She studied graphic design at Busan National University, one of South Korea's leading institutions, and was a student at the illustration school HILLS. Her cast of colorful characters comes together in an amalgam of painting and collage to form narratives for children to immerse themselves in. The young artist has already published several books that have begun to reach international audiences. These days, Kim creates not only children's books, but also works in various fields of illustration, such as advertisements, bilboards, and illustrations for periodicals.

1

3

Törnrosa [2,3]
Author/Illustrator Charles Perrault/Lena Sjöberg
First Published 2009, Rabén & Sjögren, Sweden
Original Language Swedish

2

Vad har du bakom ryggen? [1,4]
Author/Illustrator Lena Sjöberg
First Published 2012, Rabén & Sjögren, Sweden
Original Language Swedish

lena sjöberg

Swedish author and illustrator Lena Sjöberg has written over 10 children's books. In addition, she runs her own publishing house called Ritförlaget, through which she publishes non-commercial books in small editions. One of these books, *Hur får man en idé, egentligen?* (2009), was also printed in English as *How to Get an Idea*. Many of her books are also published by larger publishing houses, such as the recent *Vad har du bakom ryggen?* (Rabén & Sjögren, 2012), and *Tank om ...* (Rabén & Sjögren, 2010). Whether published in a small edition or distributed widely, her books are consistently thoughtful and funny. Sjöberg lives with her family in the Swedish countryside.

En SKATT!

Tiny Little Fly [1]
Author/Illustrator Michael Rosen/Kevin Waldron
First Published 2010, Walker Books, United Kingdom
Original Language English

The Owl and the Pussycat [2,3,5]
Author/Illustrator Edward Lear/Kevin Waldron
First Published 2010, Simon & Schuster, United Kingdom
Original Language English

Mille-Mailles ne veut plus tricoter [4]
Author/Illustrator Valérie Cros/Kevin Waldron
First Published 2010, Pomme d'Api, France
Original Language French

kevin waldron

Kevin Waldron was born in 1979 in Dublin. After living in London for several years, he ended up in New York, where he now lives and works. Waldron's first picture book was *Mr. Peek and the Misunderstanding at the Zoo,* published by Templar in 2010. In 2011, he was given the great honor of the Bull-Bransom Award for his collaborative effort *Tiny Little Fly,* written by Michael Rosen. The award recognizes excellence in children's book illustration with a focus on wildlife and nature. The book tells the story of a tiny fly who out-smarts much larger animals, rendered by Waldron in bold, colorful, double-page spreads.

3

1

The Ice Party [1]
Author/Illustrator Lynette Evans/Annie Wilkinson
First Published 2013, Macmillan, New Zealand
Original Language English

Untitled [2,3,4]
Author/Illustrator Annie Wilkinson
Personal Works

annie wilkinson

The youngest of eight children, Annie Wilkinson was raised in Saskatchewan, Canada. A self-taught artist, her illustration career began rather unexpectedly when she was given her first illustration job after applying to be the company's Web designer. This led to contract work for Robeez baby shoes and then to a diverse range of projects. As a freelance illustrator, Wilkinson creates a variety of work for everything from flash games to children's books, using traditional mediums such as oil pastel, watercolors, marker, and also digitally, using Paintbook, Adobe Illustrator, and Photoshop.

Ti Poucet [1,3]
Author/Illustrator Stéphane Servant/Ilya Green
First Published 2009,
Editions Rue du Monde, France
Original Language French

Achille et la rivière [4]
Author/Illustrator Olivier Adam/Ilya Green
First Published 2011, Actes Sud, France
Original Language French

Les Rêves racontés aux petits curieux [2]
Author/Illustrator Sylvie Beaussier/Ilya Green
First Published 2009, Syros, France
Original Language French

ilya green

A native of France's Provence region, Ilya Green was born in 1976. She studied literature and began writing at a young age. Green's books, such as *Achille et la rivière* (Actes Sud Junior, 2011) and *Le Pestacle* (Didier Jeunesse, 2010), provide a unique and often quirky take on childhood. A graduate of the National School of Fine Arts in Paris, Green collaborates with diverse authors, creating beautiful images for a wide range of publishers and clients. Green creates her vibrant, detailed illustrations using various mixed-media techniques: primarily collage, acrylic on acetate, and colored pencil.

Alice au pays des merveilles [1]
Author/Illustrator Lewis Caroll/Gaëlle Duhazé
Personal Work 2009, Image for the exhibition
"Eat Me, Drink Me," Galerie l'Art de Rien, Paris

Le Petit Roi [2]
Illustrator Gaëlle Duhazé
Personal Work 2009

Homme-Requin [3,4]
Author/Illustrator Shen Qifeng/Gaëlle Duhazé
First Published 2009, HongFei Cultures, France

gaëlle duhazé

French artist Gaëlle Duhazé has a degree in art history, but is self-taught in terms of artistic expression. An illustrator not only of children's books but of various commercial products, CD covers, and advertisements, she has developed her own pictorial universe inhabited by spirits and organic forms with a unique sensibility and humor. Inspired by diverse influences such as Japanese and Chinese folk art, Duhazé often creates and publishes under the name Perdita Corleone. Her fantastic work can currently be seen on a wide range of products by Monoprix – including chocolate cereal, yogurt, and shampoo. Duhazé was born in 1979 and currently lives and works in the region of Angoulême, France.

2

3

Untitled [1,2,4]
Illustrator Elsa Klever
Illustrations 2012

Leidenschaft und Disziplin: Kirsten Boies Kinder- und Jugendbücher 1985–2010 [3]
Illustrator Elsa Klever
First Published 2010, BibSpider, Germany
Original Language German

elsa klever

Elsa Klever was born in Berlin in 1985. Inspired and influenced by music, coffee, oddities, people's dreams, her own visions, the colors of autumn, and little furry animals, she creates her own small illustrated worlds – playful and colorful, with just a hint of weirdness. Throughout her studies at the Hamburg University of Applied Science and the Lucerne University of Applied Science and Arts (Switzerland), she developed her own visual language and style using pigmented watercolors. Elsa has worked for several magazines and corporations and has participated in various international exhibitions, for example, in Bologna, Tokyo, Lucerne, and of course Hamburg, where she lives and works as a freelance illustrator.

Comment la mort est revenue à la vie [1,2]
Author/Illustrator Muriel Bloch / Atak
First Published 2007, Editions Thierry Magnier, France
Original Language French

Verrückte Welt [3,4]
Author/Illustrator Atak
First Published 2009, JacobiStuart, Germany
Original Language German

atak

ATAK was born in 1967 as Georg Barber, in Frankfurt, Germany. He gave his first comic-book series the fitting title *Wondertüte*, meaning "surprise bag," a term which could be equally applied to his entire oeuvre – illustrations, objects, installations, prints, and comics. He has taught at various institutions in Europe and has held solo exhibitions in cities such as Paris, Berlin, Stockholm, and Helsinki. ATAK is now mainly occupied with creating kid's books. To celebrate the 200th anniversary of Heinrich Hoffman, ATAK, together with comic artist Fil, brought back to life one of the most successful German children's books, Struwwelpeter (Ken & Aber, 2009).

Comment la mort est revenue à la vie
Author/Illustrator Muriel Bloch/Atak
First Published 2007, Éditions Thierry Magnier, France
Original Language French

interview claire walters on the educational aspects of children's picture books

(Former) primary school teacher, magazine editor, and children's book author Claire Walters prefers a light-hearted, playful touch when it comes to imparting information to her adoring preschool fans. And proves that there is no need to choose between well-meant yet dry pedagogic tomes and silly stories when you want to stimulate your kid's intellect and imagination.

FREQUENTLY WRITTEN AND DEVELOPED TOGETHER WITH LONG-TERM COLLABORATOR AND FELLOW EDITOR JANE KEMP, WALTERS' AFFECTING AND AFFECTIONATE STORIES, GAMES, AND INSPIRATIONS—OFTEN WITH AN EDUCATIONAL TWIST—HIGHLIGHT THE VALUE OF FRUITFUL COOPERATIONS AND A GROUNDING IN CHILD DEVELOPMENT TO GET THE APPEALING RESULT JUST RIGHT FOR PARENTS AND CHILDREN ALIKE. FIRST THINGS FIRST: WHAT IS YOUR PROFESSIONAL BACKGROUND—AND WHAT INSPIRED YOU TO WRITE YOUR OWN CHILDREN'S BOOKS?

After school, I trained as a primary school teacher and for a number of years I taught an infant class of six- to seven-year-olds, which I much enjoyed. Later, I worked in publishing, first in books and then in magazines, finally ending up in the features department of *Practical Parenting*—a British magazine for parents of preschool children—in the 1990s. I had always had an interest in children's literature, setting up a small library at the primary school in which I worked, but soon I was able to expand my interest in this area by becoming a regular book reviewer for the magazine. Here, a colleague—Jane Kemp—and I also had the chance to devise a series of books for babies and young children that was connected to the magazine, and that launched our joint writing career.
At the same time, although I love to write children's books, I have always earned my living principally as a journalist, working for mainstream women's magazines. So the two have always gone in tandem. In addition to picture books for preschool children, Jane and I have written several screenplays for children's TV programs, such as *Balamory*, a BBC Scotland production, and a number of books for parents on games and activities to play with their children. Also, I have an unfulfilled ambition to write a longer story for older children of around nine to ten years old—but at the moment, that is only a germ of an idea.

COULD YOU TAKE US THROUGH YOUR JOINT CREATIVE PROCESS? HOW DOES YOUR COLLABORATION WITH JANE WORK IN PRACTICE?

Usually, one of us will come up with an initial idea, which we then work on together, usually at our kitchen tables or in a café. Our approach is quite visual, sketching out a miniature dummy and seeing how the basic plot might progress throughout the book and then adding a working text by hand. Afterwards, we type up simple descriptions of the images on display and refine the text so that it reads more elegantly and fluently. Of course, once it comes to the official editorial process, certain aspects of the book may change to accommodate the practical requirements of an individual publisher. In terms of pictures, we do not choose the illustrators—that is down to the publisher. But we are shown illustrator roughs and invited to add our comments on these. And we do occasionally meet our illustrators.

AS FEATURES EDITORS OF A PARENTING MAGAZINE (AND A FORMER SCHOOL TEACHER), YOU HAVE FIRST-HAND INSIGHTS INTO THE INS AND OUTS OF PARENTING AND CHILD DEVELOPMENT. HOW DOES THIS KNOWLEDGE AND BACKGROUND AFFECT YOUR STORYLINES AND THE WAY YOU APPROACH PICTURE BOOKS IN GENERAL?

At *Practical Parenting*, we were very lucky to have worked with a wide range of experts in their field, from child health practitioners to psychologists, educationalists, and parenting gurus, and this has undoubtedly informed our writing. We know, for instance, that young children love rhythm, rhyme, and repetition—and that they respond well to humor, especially when it is the adult rather than the child making a mistake!

AT THE SAME TIME, THERE SEEMS TO BE A STRONG EMPHASIS ON LEARNING AND EXPLORATION. IS THERE ALWAYS AN UNDERLYING MESSAGE TO BE UNEARTHED?

Young children learn through everything they do and experience. Of course that is mostly to do with their daily interactions, but they can also explore new ideas vicariously through books. Sometimes, we have been asked to write something specifically educational, such as an alphabet or number

Verrückte Welt
Author/Illustrator Atak
First Published 2009, JacobiStuart, Germany
Original Language German

book like *Ten Sleepy Bunnies*, but at other times we just write a story for the fun of it. However, I guess we do still try to emphasize certain values, such as kindness, generosity, and fairness.

WHAT HAS WRITING CHILDREN'S BOOKS (AND THEIR RECEPTION) TAUGHT YOU ABOUT PRESCHOOL KIDS—AND YOURSELF?

I think it is more the other way round—we tend to learn from the preschool kids! Young children are effortlessly inventive and creative, and several of our books have been inspired by observing our own or friends' children, such as with *Busy Babies Go Swimming* or *I Very Really Miss You*, where a boy misses his brother while he is away on a school trip. I would never claim to know what a child is thinking as it is impossible to get inside another person's head. But you can observe how a child behaves and watch how he approaches a problem, makes a friend, or laughs at something he finds funny—and you can incorporate these observations into your own work.

MOVING FROM THEORY TO PRACTICE, HOW DO YOU "ROAD TEST" YOUR NEW CREATIONS?

Between us, we have six children, so in the past we usually tried our stories out on them and simply used them as "guinea pigs." Now, mostly, they are grown up—which means we have to borrow friends' and relatives' children to road test our ideas.

GENERALLY SPEAKING, WHAT MAKES IMAGES SO EFFECTIVE AS A STORYTELLING DEVICE?

Every day, we all process a vast amount of visual information. Even very young children quickly become adept at picking up on visual clues, from facial expressions to objects that are only half glimpsed, such as the tail of a cat up in a tree. In a picture book, where the visual information is of course two- rather than three-dimensional, the artist skilfully directs the reader's attention to what matters by distilling the story into a short series of images that are shown in sequence to create meaning. He or she then uses pictorial devices such as line, color, composition, and framing to delineate character and add emotional resonance. As the critic and teacher Jane Doonan has pointed out, in *Looking at Pictures in Picture Books*, "every mark displayed in a picture is a potential carrier of meaning".

In terms of style or storyline, there is such an enormous range of children's picture books, covering a wide breadth of subjects and aimed at such a variety of ages, that it is impossible to pin down one particular approach. Generally speaking, I suppose, many books have a circular, or rather spiral, structure whereby the ending reflects the beginning, but in a slightly different way. The protagonist is usually on some sort of emotional journey and returns to his original position with new insights. However, just as with books for adults, each book is likely to have its own internal logic, which may vary considerably from one title to another.

LET'S TALK ABOUT THE CONCEPT OF "BOOKS FROM BIRTH." FROM WHAT AGE DO BOOKS ACTUALLY MAKE SENSE? HOW DOES THE PERCEPTION AND USE OF PICTURE BOOKS CHANGE BETWEEN THE AGES OF ZERO AND THE FIRST DAY OF SCHOOL?

I think you can use books with babies pretty much from the first month. Newborns are attracted to strong outlines, sharp contrasts, and images with clearly defined edges, so black and white board books work well with this age group. As they get older, babies enjoy looking at realistic and colorful images of objects they recognize and love books that involve expressive sounds, such as animal or vehicle noises. By the time they are toddlers, they are beginning to make sense of much more detailed pictures and can enjoy simple storylines as well as fun novelty elements such as flaps and pages that open up into bigger pictures. And when they enter nursery at around three or four years old, if they have been exposed to books from early on, they can follow quite complex storylines and interpret highly detailed images. Plus, of course, they are learning a great deal of practical information about how books in Western culture work, with stories reading from the front to the back of the book, from the top to the bottom of the page, and with words reading from left to right.

KINDNESS, GENEROSITY, AND FAIRNESS.

SPEAKING OF WORDS AND "READING," HOW DO WORDLESS PICTURE BOOKS DIFFER FROM REGULAR CHILDREN'S BOOKS? BOTH IN THE WAY THAT YOU, AS AUTHORS, MIGHT APPROACH THEIR CREATION AND THE WAY THEY ARE USED BY CHILDREN AND THEIR GUARDIANS?

Jane and I have never actually created any wordless books ourselves, but I have a personal interest in this subject because I wrote the dissertation for my recent master's in children's literature on it. Wordless picture books differ from books with verbal text by virtue of the fact that meaning in them is created entirely through the visual images. That is not to say there isn't a story there, rather that the story has to be recreated by the reader through an examination and interpretation of the pictures.

DO KIDS THEMSELVES APPROACH THESE BOOKS DIFFERENTLY? DO THEY FIND THEIR OWN WAY THROUGH THE STORY, DEVELOP ALTERNATIVE NARRATIVES, OR EVEN TELL THE STORY TO THEIR PARENTS, THUS REVERSING ROLES?

Reading a wordless picture book is usually a demanding process, and children often find it tiring, so parents may need to be patient and encouraging. But the experience can be deeply rewarding as the reader invests considerable time and energy in recreating the plot and the characters, and may eventually come to have a sense of ownership over them. Some books have quite simple storylines that result in surprisingly similar interpretations, while others are so open-ended that they can have multiple, even infinite, interpretations.

FINALLY, WHERE DO YOU SEE CHILDREN'S BOOKS GOING IN THE FUTURE?

There are many exciting new developments in graphic novels for children, such as Brian Selznick's *The Invention of Hugo Cabret* (later made into the film *Hugo*), and in digital publishing, for instance *The Fantastic Flying Books of Mr. Morris Lessmore* by William Joyce and Brandon Oldenburg, which is available as an animated film, an app, and soon a picture book (late 2012). The jury is out on how these new forms are going to progress, but personally I think there will always be a place for the traditional picture book. A good plot, well told and sensitively illustrated in print, is always going to have an appeal. A fact reflected in the continued popularity of best-selling picture book classics like the late Maurice Sendak's *Where The Wild Things Are*, Eric Carle's *The Very Hungry Caterpillar* and Pat Hutchins's *Rosie's Walk*, or in the success of more recent and innovative publications such as Julia Donaldson and Axel Scheffler's *The Gruffalo* or Lauren Child's Charlie and Lola books. Children – and adults – have always loved stories and will continue to do so, in whatever format they are presented.

Nemorino und das Bündel des Narren
Author/Illustrator Chrigel Farner
First Published 2012, Salis, Germany
Original Language German

chrigel farner

Born in 1975, Chrigel Farner grew up in the Swiss village of Seuzach. He was trained in scientific illustration at the Zurich University of Applied Sciences, learning to sketch brain surgeries and cockroach anatomies. Eventually, he began to draw from his imagination, resulting in a number of comic short stories, a comic book, and numerous illustrations. Since then, Farner has worked as a freelance illustrator, cartoonist, and painter in Zurich and Berlin. His illustrations geared toward children demonstrate the same keen eye, hilarious sense of humor, and slightly dark wit as his work made for adults.

Adam and Eve [3]
Author/Illustrator Alicia Baladan
Unpublished 2012

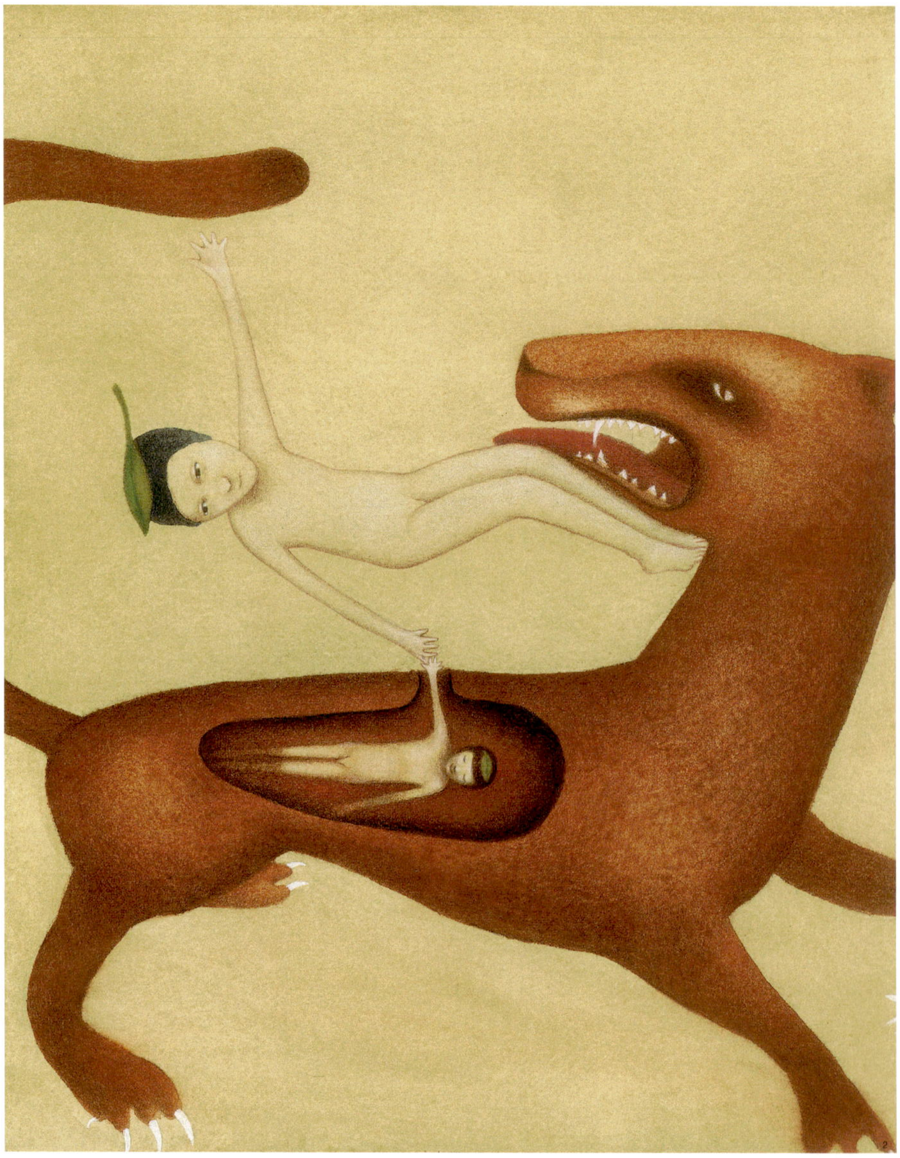

Una storia guaranì [1,2,5]
Author/Illustrator Alicia Baladan
First Published 2010, Topipittori, Italy
Original Language Italian

Cuentos del globo 2: De bellas y bestias [4]
Illustrator Alicia Baladan
First Published 2012, Pequeño editor, Argentina
Original Language Spanish

alicia baladan

Alicia Baladan was born in 1969 in Uruguay, where she lived until she was 11. After finishing school in Rio de Janeiro, she moved to Italy, where she graduated from the Academy of Fine Arts of Brera in Milan. Currently living in Brescia, Italy, Baladan has participated in several exhibitions and international film festivals with her animations and experimental movies. She has also collaborated with Stalker Multimedia in the realization of cultural projects and exhibitions in various museums. For several years, Baladan has concentrated on illustration, developing the narrative aspect of her visual work. *Una storia guarani* was her first book.

La Colère de Banshee [2,3]
Author/Illustrator Jean-François Chabas/David Sala
First Published 2010, Casterman, France
Original Language French

Le Coffre enchanté [1,4]
Author/Illustrator Jean-François Chabas/David Sala
First Published 2011, Casterman, France
Original Language French

david sala

Currently living in the city of Nimes, France, David Sala is originally from Lyon, where he was born in 1973. He attended the prestigious Emile Cohl School of Arts, and after finishing his studies he started to work as an illustrator. He mainly did covers for science-fiction books, sword-and-sorcery, and crime fiction. The next step in his career was to illustrate children's books – and then he began to work in comics, where his love for drawing, narrative, and color finds its way into his wonderful art. Sala has been widely recognized for his talents since his very first comic was released; awards include the Sérignan City Award for *Replay* in 2000 and the Albert Uderzo Award for Best Young Artist in 2002.

Les Poings sur les îles
Author/Illustrator Elise Fontenaille/Violeta Lopiz
First Published 2011, Editions du Rouergue, France
Original Language French

violeta lopiz

Hailing from the Spanish island of Ibiza and currently based in Madrid, Violeta Lopiz creates illustrations that are unmistakably retro-inspired yet modern. Her illustrations convey subject matter as complex as finance and business – in newspapers and magazines like the *Economist* and *El Mundo* – and as simple and meaningful as stories for children's books. Her most recent book for kids is called *Les poings sur les îles*, a collaboration with the French author Elise Fontenaille filled with rich colors and lush, delicate textures. Published by Le Rouergue in 2011, the book was selected as a finalist for the Korean CJ Picture Book Award.

Hyacinthe et Rose
Author/Illustrator François Morel/Martin Jarrie
First Published 2010, Éditions Thierry Magnier, France
Original Language French

martin jarrie

An artist and illustrator, Martin Jarrie has lived and worked in Paris since 1981. Beginning with a hyper-realistic style, he developed a freer type of expression, a pictorial style influenced by Surrealism and primitive art. He works for the press, publishing, and advertising, mostly in France and the United States, including projects for *Le Monde*, *Le Nouvel Observateur*, and the *New Yorker*. His illustrations have received numerous awards from *Communication Arts* and the Society of Illustrators. His book *L'Alphabet fabuleux* (Gallimard) was the winner of Best French Books 2007. His latest book, *Hyacinthe et Rose* (Thierry Magnier, 2010), received a special mention at the Bologna Children's Book Fair.

Alessandro Sanna
www.alessandrosanna.com
pages 50 / 51

Alicia Baladan
www.aliciabaladan.blogspot.com
pages 230 / 231

Amrei Fiedler
www.spatzundhirn.de
pages 206 / 207

Ana Ventura
www.anaventura.com
pages 104 / 105

Anne-Lise Boutin
www.anneliseboutin.blogspot.com
pages 102 / 103

Annelore Parot
anneloreparot.ultra-book.com
pages 78 / 79

Annie Wilkinson
www.anniewilkinson.com
pages 214 / 215

Antoine Guilloppé
www.antoine-guilloppe.com
pages 144 / 145

Atak
www.fcatak.de
pages 222 - 227

Beatrice Alemagna
www.beatricealemagna.com
pages 202 / 203

Benjamin Chaud
cyberbenjamin@wanadoo.fr
pages 56 / 57

Bernardo Carvalho
www.planetatangerina.com
pages 12 / 13

Bhajju Shyam, Durga Bai,
Ram Singh Urveti
www.tarabooks.com
pages 142 / 143

Bjørn R. Lie
www.bjornlie.com
pages 204 / 205

Blanca Gómez
www.cosasminimas.com
pages 88 / 89

Blexbolex
pages 108 / 109

Britta Teckentrup
www.brittateckentrup.com
pages 86 / 87

Camilla Engman
www.camillaengman.com
pages 196 / 197

Cecilia Afonso Esteves
www.unaflordepapel.blogspot.de
pages 146 / 147

Chad Geran
www.geran.ca
page 90

Chiara Armellini
www.chiararmellini.com
pages 136 / 137

Cho Sunkyung
www.somebooks.kr
pages 130 / 131

Chris Haughton
www.vegetablefriedrice.com
pages 98 / 99

Chrigel Farner
www.contours-art.de
pages 228 / 229

Christian Montenegro
www.christianmontenegro.com.ar
pages 80 / 81

Christopher Corr
www.christophercorr.com
pages 54 / 55

Cristian Turdera
www.cristianturdera.com
pages 194 / 195

Dajung Kim
www.dadasee.com
pages 208 / 209

Daniele Melani
www.morgangaynin.com/melani
pages 68 / 69

David Sala
www.davidsala.com
pages 232 / 233

Einar Turkowski
www.einarturkowski.de
pages 192 / 193

Elisa Géhin
www.mesjeudisamusants.fr
pages 48 / 49

Elsa Klever
www.elsaklever.de
pages 220 / 221

Emiliano Ponzi
www.emilianoponzi.com
pages 26 / 27

Emmanuelle Houdart
charte.repertoire.free.fr/h/houdart.html
pages 184 / 185

Eric Giriat
www.ericgiriat.com
pages 134 / 135

Fabrice Houdry/Yaralt
fabricehoudry.blogspot.fr
pages 110 / 111

Fereshteh Najafi
www.fereshtehnajafi.com
pages 170 / 171

Frank Viva
www.vivaandco.com
pages 64 / 65

Gaëlle Duhazé
perditacorleone.canalblog.com
pages 218 / 219

Gary Taxali
www.garytaxali.com
pages 66 / 67

Gémeo Luis
www.gemeoluis.com
pages 116 / 117

Gerry Turley
www.gerryturley.com
pages 22 / 23

Gonçalo Viana
www.goncaloviana.com
pages 84 / 85

Gry Moursund
www.cappelendamm.no
pages 52 / 53

Gwénola Carrère
www.illustrissimo.fr
pages 14 / 15

Helen J.B. Lee
blog.naver.com/helenjblee
pages 182 / 183

Ianna Andréadis
ianna.online.fr
pages 152 / 153

Ilya Green
www.ilya-green.com
pages 216 / 217

Isabelle Vandenabeele
www.eenhoorn.be
pages 178 / 179

Isidro Ferrer
www.isidroferrer.com
pages 164 / 165

index of illustrators

Joëlle Jolivet
www.joellejolivet.com
pages 176 / 177

Juanjo G. Oller
www.milimbo.com
pages 112 / 113

Judith Drews
www.byjudith.blogspot.com
pages 44 / 45

Julie Morstad
www.juliemorstad.com
pages 30 / 31

Kaatje Vermeire
www.kaatjevermeire.be
pages 198 / 199

Kevin Vanwonterghem
www.kevinvanwonterghem.be
pages 180 / 181

Kevin Waldron
www.kevinwaldron.co.uk
pages 212 / 213

Kitty Crowther
www.ecoledesloisirs.fr
pages 32 - 39, 120 - 123

Laura Varsky
www.lauravarsky.com.ar
pages 82 / 83

Laurent Moreau
zeroendictee.free.fr
pages 60 / 61

Lena Sjöberg
www.lenasjoberg.com
pages 210 / 211

Lorena Siminovich
www.lorenasiminovich.com
page 91

Lorenzo Mattotti
www.mattotti.com
pages 128 / 129

Louis Rigaud
www.ludocube.fr
pages 72 / 73

Marc Boutavant
www.heartagency.com
pages 2, 94 / 95

Maren Amini
www.maren-amini.de
pages 40 / 41

Mariana Chiesa
www.marianachiesa.blogspot.com
pages 118 / 119

Marion Billet
www.marionbillet.com
pages 92 / 93

Marjolaine Leray
www.marjolaineleray.com
pages 124 / 125

Marta Ignerska
www.martaignerska.art.pl
pages 114 / 115

Marta Madureira
www.martamadureira.com
pages 28 / 29

Martin Jarrie
www.martinjarrie.com
pages 236 / 237

Monika Hanulak
www.wytwornia.com
pages 106 / 107

Morteza Zahedi
www.mortezahedi.com
pages 172 / 173

Narges Mohammadi
nargesmohammadi.blogspot.com
pages 168 / 169

Nicola Killen
www.nicolakillen.com
pages 20 / 21

Nicolas Gouny
www.la-parenthese-enchantee.fr
pages 58 / 59

Oliver Jeffers
www.oliverjeffers.com
pages 16 / 17

Owen Davey
www.owendavey.com
pages 62 / 63

Page Tsou
www.pagetsou.com
pages 166 / 167

Philip Giordano
www.philip-giordano-pilipo.com
pages 132 / 133

Ragnar Aalbu
www.ragnaraalbu.com
pages 24 / 25

Rambharos Jha
www.tarabooks.com
pages 138 / 139

Raphael Urwiller
www.raphaelurwiller.com
pages 70 / 71

Rilla Alexander
www.byrilla.com
pages 5, 42 / 43

Sandrine Thommen
sandrinethommen.ultra-book.com
pages 140 / 141

Sarah Dyer
www.sarahdyer.com
pages 148 / 149

Satu Kontinen
www.facebook.com/satukala
www.satukala.com
pages 100 / 101

Serge Bloch
www.sergebloch.net
pages 150 / 151

Simona Mulazzani
www.morgangaynin.com/mulazzani
pages 200 / 201

Stina Wirsén
www.brokiga.se
pages 46 / 47

Sybille Schenker
www.cargocollective.com/sybille
pages 126 / 127

Tom Schamp
www.tomschamp.com
pages 74 - 77

Tomas Ives
www.tomas-ives.com
pages 174 / 175

Valeria Petrone
www.valeriapetrone.com
pages 18 / 19

Vincent Mathy
www.flickr.com/photos/vincentmathy
pages 96 / 97

Violeta Lopiz
www.violetalopiz.com
pages 234 / 235

Vitali Konstantinov
www.pittore.de
pages 190 / 191

Wolf Erlbruch
pages 154 / 155

little big books
illustrations for children's picture books

This book was conceived, edited, and designed by Gestalten.

Edited by Hendrik Hellige and Robert Klanten

Layout by Hendrik Hellige and Claire Besset
Typeface: Engel New Serif by Sofie Beier, foundry: www.gestaltenfonts.com
Introduction and interviews by Sonja Commentz
Illustrator portraits by Elvia Wilk
Cover image from *Alba Blabla & Moi* by Alex Cousseau and Anne-Lise Boutin,
© 2011 Éditions du Rouergue

Project management by Julian Sorge
Production management by Martin Bretschneider
Proofreading by Transparent Language Solutions
Printed by Optimal Media GmbH, Röbel | Made in Germany

Published by Gestalten, Berlin 2012 | ISBN 978-3-89955-446-5

3rd printing, 2014

For more information, please visit www.gestalten.com.

Bibliographic information published by the Deutsche Nationalbibliothek. The Deutsche Nationalbibliothek lists this publication in the Deutsche Nationalbibliografie; detailed bibliographic data are available online at http://dnb.d-nb.de.

None of the content in this book was published in exchange for payment by commercial parties or designers; Gestalten selected all included work based solely on its artistic merit.

This book was printed according to the internationally accepted ISO 14001 standards for environmental protection, which specify requirements for an environmental management system.

This book was printed on paper certified by the FSC®.

FSC www.fsc.org MIX Paper from responsible sources FSC® C108521

Gestalten is a climate-neutral company. We collaborate with the non-profit carbon offset provider myclimate (www.myclimate.org) to neutralize the company's carbon footprint produced through our worldwide business activities by investing in projects that reduce CO_2 emissions (www.gestalten.com/myclimate).

myclimate
Protect our planet